Where I've Been
Dan Heiser

This book is dedicated to all those who
served their countries during World
War I:
July 1914 – November 1918.

Acknowledgements:
I want to start off by thanking my parents, Diane and Jim Heiser. I want to personally thank them for watching all the documentaries I had found on World War I with me. Without their support I feel this book would have never seen the light of day. I also want to thank Christian Saunders who gave his time to edit and give me excellent feedback. Lastly I want to thank Greg Chapman who without him I probably would still be struggling to find an incredible artist like him.

Table of Contents

Chapter 1

The spring of 1917 brought an era of change. It was a quiet evening. The sun was on the verge of setting and Edward lay in the grass under the old sycamore, staring at the sky waiting for the first of the stars to come out. He was a handsome young lad, with sandy blond hair kept tight and short. His coral blue eyes grew heavy as he stared into the twilight. He smiled as he closed his eyes, absently scratching his clean-shaven chin. Taking a deep breath he inhaled the sweet early spring air.

"What are you doing?" a soft female voice broke the silence.

He opened his eyes, and looked at a young seventeen-year-old girl. She was fragile and pure, her soft pale skin showed her innocent glow. Her autumn red hair was braided and tied in a bun.

"Waiting for the stars," Edward answered, returning his gaze to the sky. She stood awkwardly before him, her silence was deafening. "I don't want you worrying," he sighed.

"Worrying," she laughed weakly.

"Christine," he sighed sitting up and giving her the attention she was seeking. "What else do you want of me?"

"I want you to stay? I want you to stay with me."

He stood up, realizing he wouldn't get the peace he wanted.

"Your birthday is supposed to be a joyous celebration but you treat it as a death sentence and throw those that love you to the wind," she winced covering her mouth.

"Christine," he sighed reaching out to her. She recoiled a little before finally taking his hand. "You know I love you, you are my life, you are my breath. We have said it a hundred times. But we are at war."

"We aren't, Eddie," she whined grabbing him under the chin. "We aren't. Look, what do you see?" She turned his face to the small cottages of their small little town. "I don't see war. I see a quaint little town, secluded to their own being."

"And would you tell that to Mrs. Brady?" he asked. "Who lost not just her husband but her oldest son?"

"Well…"

"Or Mr. and Mrs. Smithy? Who still haven't heard from their boy?"

"Edward," she sighed.

"Or… my mother," he paused thinking of his father who was apart of a battalion that never returned home. "Don't think of the day that comes after tomorrow, nor think of the day of tomorrow. Think of now as I stand before you in my very flesh," he whispered before giving her a quick kiss. She smiled and he guided her down the hill back to their village. A million thoughts ran through his head as Christine talked to him, painting a future of what she thought the world would be when the War to End All Wars was over. She pictured a lovely world but Edward's thoughts were not with hers.

Excitement and fear ran through his veins as he thought of the day after his eighteenth birthday.

His brother Andrew, six years older than him, was already in France flying above the country taking the Germans out of the sky. He wanted to be a pilot like him, but felt the war would be ending before he had the chance.

As they reached the edge of town Christine kissed his cheek and said her goodbye and returned home. Edward walked down the street, the quiet evening relaxing him once more. He passed through town and walked down the old dirt trail leading to an old looking barn next to a large cottage. A few lights illuminated the house. He walked into the barn the smell of damp wood and horse dung filled his nostrils. To some, this smell would put off. But Edward was far too used to it.

He stopped before the last stall at the end and sucked on his cheek as a black horse crept forward into the light. He smiled as he made eye contact with the animal's chocolate eyes. He named her Frosty Queen, for the white spot around her eye and the fact she was born on the coldest night of the year. She was three now, and Edward took good care of her.

"How are ya holding girl?" he whispered petting her nose as she sniffed his hand for a carrot. "I don't have anything for ya," he laughed as she started nibbling at his shirt. "No... up, wait," he laughed as she tugged at his shirt. "Could this be what ya smell?" he laughed pulling out a carrot from under his shirt. Frosty Queen whinnied and took the carrot from his hand.

"She's a good horse," a masculine voice called out.

"She is, isn't she Andrew?" Edward laughed as Frosty Queen nudged him for more. "Andrew?" Edward questioned cocking his head back as he looked at his brother at the end of the barn. His feet were ahead of his mind as he ran toward his brother nearly tackling him as he hugged him. "What are you...?"

"What am I doing home?" Andrew laughed.

Edward looked at his brother funny. "I'm only here till the day after tomorrow. I'm here to enlist more men." Andrew shook his head. "You're too young," Andrew sighed. "Come, mother's probably waiting with dinner," he added putting his hand on Edward's shoulder.

Edward forced himself to nod and said goodnight to his horse before following his brother. Andrew stood frozen before the front door. "I don't know about this."

"Know about what?" Edward asked as he opened the front door. "Hello, who's home?" he shouted as two little kids came running down the stairs. Both his sister and brother hugged him, his sister reaching his waste and his brother wrapping around his leg. "Hey," Edward whispered as the little boy looked up from the floor.

"Andrew!" their sister shouted, releasing Edward and rushing to her older brother's side. "You're home!" she screamed.

"Hello, Lily," Andrew chuckled, picking up the seven year old. The little boy, no older than three, still clung to Edward's leg and looked at Andrew as if he was a foreigner.

"Who that?" the boy asked looking at Edward uncertainly.

"That's Andrew. He's your brother," Edward laughed, lifting Will off the ground.

"You brother," Will said poking Edward as he looked at Andrew.

"Mum?" Andrew called out as Edward looked behind him and spotted his mother standing in the doorway of the kitchen wiping her hands with a rag.

"Thank God," the older woman whispered, briskly walking down the hall and embracing her son. "Thank God," she whispered again as Edward watched his brother fighting back tears.

The family of five stood in silence for a few minutes. The world seemed to have stopped for them in that moment. The rest of the night following dinner, Andrew shared his stories as an ace fighter pilot and how many Germans he'd taken down over the countryside of France. The time seemed endless. Twilight turned to night and the night grew late, and for once the house slept as it had before Andrew left for the war.

At dawn on March 10, 1917 the sound of William and Lily knocking on his door woke Edward. He looked out the window at the rising sun and smiled widely. Sitting on the edge of his bed, he grabbed the small picture of his father and looked at it for a moment.

"I miss ya, Dad," he whispered, before placing the picture back on his end table. Quickly he changed from his silk pajamas into his heavy cotton riding clothes. Opening his door, he found Will holding his riding boots.

"Frosty Queen, Frosty Queen," said Will excitedly as Edward took the boots from his baby brother.

"Thank you," he laughed, patting the child on the head before forcing his feet into his boots.

"Happy… Birthday," Lily called as Edward was already running down the stairs.

"Thank you, Lily," he called back to the little girl, "I'll be right back," he added rushing to the barn. Saddling Frosty Queen he guided his horse from the barn and quickly hurdled himself up on her back. "Come on girl, onward," he shouted, tapping her sides with his heels. She gave a quick whinny before trotting up the road. He dug his heals into Frosty Queen's side as she started into a gallop, holding the reins tight and staying low as she jumped over a fallen tree.

The freedom made him not think of what the day would bring, or what the war held. In that moment he was free, free from war, free from people and stress and looking after his family. Edward was his own man, and that's what he was in the eyes of the law, a man.

Over the rolling hills past the misting ponds, the morning seemed to be alive and well. Edward knew nothing of where he was going or where he was leading his horse. He tasted the freedom and let his mind run free, along with his heart. He looked at the sky, wanting to see the world from the heavens.

Suddenly and without warning, Frosty Queen skidded to a halt, throwing Edward from the saddle. His moment of flight faded from his mind as he flew through the air. Landing on his shoulder, he rolled a few feet.

Frosty Queen neighed in fear before jumping and galloping away in fright. "Queenie!" he shouted as the horse made its retreat. Edward watched in surprise as his horse left his side. In awe and disbelief, he turned to see what had spooked her. He stared at the former shell of the small village near his. Buildings blown out and turned to rubble giving the area an ominous feeling. Roads barricaded with barbed wire told him that the people planned for an attack that may never come. He closed his eyes and could hear the engines of planes in his mind.

Slowly, he moved forward, climbing over a small stone wall that barely stood any more. The town smelled of gunpowder and the remnants of fire. For the first time, Edward realized that the war had been so close to home, and the thought began to frighten him. He placed his hand on a rotted doorframe and closed his eyes. The life was gone from the village and it saddened him. The longer he lingered, the angrier he got.

Silently he walked through a house, and then another. Irreplaceable items were scattered on the floor of each house, and Edward knew they would most likely never be recovered.

"Edward," Andrew sighed, placing his hand on Edward's shoulder causing his younger brother to scream and start swinging his fists randomly. "Edward, Edward, calm down," Andrew laughed grabbing his brother's wrists. Edward stopped but his heart pounded in his ears. "What the hell are you doing out here?"

"I... I... Frosty Queen, she brought me here," Edward said frantically trying to catch up with his racing heart. "I didn't even know this existed."

"It happened early in the war," Andrew answered quickly.

"This is why I need..."

"You can't be an ace fighter pilot," Andrew interrupted. Edward looked at Andrew sternly,

waiting for more than that answer. "You're too
young, learning would take too long."

"You know I can learn anything," Edward
said as Andrew pinched the bridge of his nose.

"Do you know chance of survival when you
go up in the air?" Andrew said calmly as Edward
studied his brother. "The chance is small and it only
keeps going down. I've been lucky myself, but
since I'm telling you, the average length of flight in
days is seventeen, Edward. Seventeen," Andrew
gritted his teeth. Edward stood quietly as he could
see the stress finally breaking his brother. The one
man he knew in his life that never gave up, never
succumbed to stress, and never broke. Edward
could tell his brother had returned to him a changed
man, a shell of his former self. "I spoke with
Christine," Andrew said when he finally gathered
himself together.

"Oh."

"And she tells me you plan on trying to sign
up tomorrow."

"She's right, and I don't plan, I am going
to."

"Edward..." Andrew sighed. Edward
watched as his brother reached into his pocket.
"Hold out your hand." He followed his brother's
orders and Andrew placed two small golden
cufflinks in his hand. "They were dad's," he said as
Edward fiddled with the trinkets. He noticed his
father's initials were inscribed on the flat part of the
cufflink. "He'd want you to make your own
decisions, I can longer treat you like a child. If this
is what you want so be it. Just promise me you
won't come to me when you sign up?"

"I promise," Edward said, still looking at the
cufflinks in his hand.

"Now, let's get back before anyone starts missing us on your birthday."

"Or have mother release the hounds and search party," Edward said as Andrew laughed.

Chapter 2

The fog was light the morning after Edward's birthday. A gloom felt thick in the air as he pulled himself from bed, his thoughts of enlisting no longer filled him with excitement, but fear. The sun was just on the horizon barely breaking the night. He washed his face and took himself to the barn. There, he found his brother Andrew brushing Frosty Queen.

"Today's going to be a long day," Andrew sighed as he paused and looked at his brother. Edward nodded silently, not knowing what to say. Frosty Queen grunted and nudged Andrew wanting him to brush her more causing both men to laugh. "We are past force enlisting. You don't have…"

"I need to do this. I want to sign up, Andrew," Edward spoke up finally. "I live for mother and Christine and the rest of the family. But I also live for my country, which means I will fight by fellow countrymen to make sure those that threaten my country are stopped." The brothers stared at each other in silence. Edward, although scared, knew what he said was true. He was ready to grow up.

"Have you told mother?"

Edward nodded slowly.

"Last week. She was expecting it, or so she told me. I don't know if I believed her or not."

"Well, there's no changing your mind."

Edward shook his head, and without saying anything further Andrew left him alone in the barn.

"You ready girl?" he whispered, rubbing her nose. He saddled Frosty Queen and trotted her out of the barn and toward town. He tugged Frosty Queen's reins to slow her down even more, letting her walk as the voices started talking in his head.

When he made it to town, he found a good few of his friends talking with each other or a recruiter. Mothers and wives stood in groups looking dreadful. This morning did bring the fog which brought the fear and mourning with it. A few people glanced at him as he climbed down from Frosty Queen.

"You're signing up too?" someone asked as he looked up to see who was speaking with him. His friend Gavin stood holding Frosty Queen's reins petting the horse with one hand. Gavin Creets was a year older than Edward and worked in the factory, which was why he hadn't enlisted earlier. Gavin was posh and knew it, and was very proud of it. He valued his appearance above all things. His blond hair was cut clean and often slicked back. He was the ladies man of town, and could capture all women with his green eyes. All except for Christine, which always seemed to bother him.

"Yeah, I'm enlisting. You come to see who else is leaving?" Edward asked as he pointed to the post behind Gavin and watched his friend tie the reins around it.

"Not exactly. If I have to build another part for these tanks I may scream," he chuckled as

Edward smirked. "I'm actually signing up to be one of the engineers for the tanks. I mean, who knows them better than those who built 'em?" he laughed as Edward nodded. Edward remained silent, his hand on Frosty Queen's neck. He was dazed by his thoughts. "You scared?"

"Terrified," he answered quietly. "You?"

Gavin nodded.

"My father used to say cowards die many times before their deaths, the valiant never taste of death but once." Edward looked at Gavin oddly. "It means…"

"I know what it means, but why quote Shakespeare?" Edward asked.

"My dad loved reading Shakespeare, and when you think about it, he often wrote the truth," Gavin shrugged, patting Frosty Queen before walking away.

Edward kissed Frosty Queen on the nose and walked toward an enlister. He glanced over at his brother who was talking with a few gentlemen probably trying to enlist them. Edward looked around the town square. There were a few uniforms he didn't recognize.

"That one your horse?" a man asked walking up to him and pointing at Frosty Queen.

"Aye," Edward answered proudly. "She's fast too, before you ask," he laughed.

"I'm guessing you've heard the cavalry is in search of horses," he said.

Edward shook his head.

"My horse isn't for sale. She just brought me here to sign up."

"You?" the man pointed at him. "Aren't you a little young? Hell, like it matters, people have been lying about their age just to get their names memorialized."

"I turned eighteen yesterday, actually," Edward said stubbornly.

"How long have you been riding?"

"Since I was five."

"You give any thought to who you wanted to enlist with."

"I have my eye on one group, and that's the ace fighter planes."

"You're a little young for that don't ya think?" the man laughed as Edward nodded, rolling his eyes. "You think of signing up with the British Army?" the man pursued.

Edward shook his head.

"Well, allow me to properly introduce myself. Lieutenant Hannah Gyles, apart of the 4th Queen's own Hussars," The man said, offering his hand for Edward to shake.

"The cavalry?" Lieutenant Gyles nodded at Edward's question. He hadn't given it much thought; in all honestly he hadn't given many divisions of the armed forces much consideration. He only had thoughts of being a pilot. "Isn't it dangerous?"

"Hell all of it's dangerous," Lieutenant Gyles laughed. "We are the ones who lead the groups beyond the lines, our bravery is our shield. The horses our priority and if your horse is as fast as you say it is, then I think you'll be the perfect fit."

Edward hesitated, shaking his head.

"Look, let me be honest."

Edward remained silent simply nodding his head.

"Your chance of being successful with any of the recruiters is slim," Lieutenant Gyles continued. "They are looking for the older men who have had some experience with life. You sign up with me, and I'll personally take you under my wing. Teach you everything you need to know. I'll even teach ya how to be a better rider. No one in the 4th is better than I," he boasted, removing his cap he ran his hand through his salt n pepper hair. For a man with grays he looked fairly young, his sparkling hazel eyes lied of his age just as much as his tight skin. "And you really can't separate an iconic duo. A man isn't a man without his horse," Gyles said as Edward looked over his shoulder at Frosty Queen who began chewing on her reins.

"Will I come home?"

For the first time since talking with Edward, Lieutenant Hannah Gyles became silent. The older man took a deep breath and crossed his arms. "I am no place to promise such a thing. But I can promise to help you and give my own life for yours as your Lieutenant," he said as Edward stood quietly for a minute before taking a deep breath and nodded.

"I'll enlist," Edward managed to say, not allowing his fear to show.

"Grand," Lieutenant Gyles said, handing Edward the paperwork. As quickly as he could he signed the papers. When he was finished, both men shook each other's hand in a mutual silence. Edward knew his life was on the verge of a great change that would take his simple existence and destroy it in one setting. He made his way over to Frosty Queen and untied her reins.

"We're a team, girl. You and me. Where you go, I go," he whispered in her ear as she breathed heavily out of her nostrils as if to agree. "I will make sure you stay safe."

"So, the cavalry?" Andrew asked. Edward closed his eyes as he tangled one of his hands in Frosty Queen's mane, sucking in his snot as he tried to not show his brother the fear.

"I'm not going to talk to you about my decisions," Edward said, his voice stern and strong, almost foreign to him.

"Edward, I..."

"Andrew, no more." Edward looked at his brother. "My entry into this war begins with Frosty Queen. A familiar face close will keep me sane," he sighed, saddling his horse. "I'll see you at the end, in this life or the next," he said saluting his brother with his right hand, fingers clenched together and palm facing outward. Andrew chuckled and stepped closer.

"Something you need to know. Recently it's been changed, you salute with your left hand," Andrew smirked as Edward nodded. "And another thing, don't salute without your cap, understood?" he pointed at Edward, who nodded again. "Now... go enjoy your last day of freedom and pray to God above you come home."

Edward tugged at his horse's reins and turned her from his brother. He was making his way in the direction of home when Gavin stepped in his path.

"Let's get a drink," Gavin proposed as Edward stopped the horse.

"I'd rather spend the day with my family, Gav," Edward said.

"Come on, one drink," Gavin smiled.

Edward knew there was no such thing as one drink with Gavin, but he also knew that this may be the last time he would be able to get a drink with his friend. He sighed and Gavin smiled, patting his friend's shoulder.

"That's what I like to hear," he laughed as Edward shook his head. Tying Frosty Queen to a post once more he followed Gavin to the pub, an old thatched building that seemed to withstand time itself. They sat in a booth in the corner that looked out upon the square. "Stout?" Gavin asked pointing at Edward who simply shook his head and held his hand up.

"I'll start with a coffee."

Gavin looked at his friend as if he was growing a second head. "You'll have a stout," he laughed before walking away. Edward chuckled and returned his gaze to the window. Gavin returned shortly and placed a dark black beer in front of Edward who would not take his eyes from the window.

"Did... did we do the right thing?" Edward finally spoke up, looking at his friend. Gavin let out of a chuckle. "No, I'm serious, Gav. What are we doing?"

"We're going to war, we were right to sign up. Think of it like this," Gavin started, placing his beer down. He reached for the salt and pepper shakers as Edward watched. "There are two kinds a people." He shook the salt and pepper at eye level. "Those that stand against the wicked and seek glory and peace for their own people. And then there are those that remain behind doing nothing more than waiting for an end. An end to nothing and an end to life," he said calmly placing the pepper down. "Now, which do you want to be? Fighting for the cause of an end to this God-awful war or a person that sits and waits? Waits for those that will never come back, wallowing in pain and regret. Eddie, we are about to make history. Our actions will shape our children's worlds."

"If we live to see them," Edward sighed, taking a deep sip of his beer.

"We'll come back stronger than we left, and so will Frosty Queen," Gavin nodded toward the window. "I saw you talking with one of the cavalry Lieutenants. I couldn't picture you doing anything else. You and that horse are inseparable," he laughed as Edward forced a chuckle. "Have you spoken to Christine?"

"Not since last night," he answered shortly. "I don't understand her, I really don't."

"What woman is understandable?" Gavin laughed drinking his pint in nearly two gulps.

"Well, that's true," Edward laughed, "but in all honesty I... don't know. One day she listens to my reasons of why I'm enlisting."

"And then at your birthday party gets drunk and starts making you feel guilty?" Gavin chuckled, although he had a long face. "You weren't the only one she made feel like crap so don't take it too personally."

"I'm not taking it personally. She was drunk... and if she wants to talk before I leave, she knows where I live."

"Even I'm saying goodbye to her," Gavin said, slightly shocked at Edward's response. "You two have..."

"Can we not talk about this? Tell me about the tanks you'll be working on," he said quickly changing the subject.

"I've been enlisted to work on one tank, the Mark IV. Honestly top of the line, better than the five. A little smaller so a smaller crew, but small is better, moves faster." Gavin went on for the next hour, talking about nearly the entire history of the Mark IV tank, naming each bolt that no one would even know the name of.

Edward sat quietly, sipping his beer listening to his friend go on. For the first time that morning, the feeling of dread and fear lifted off his shoulders. When they finished their third beer and left the pub, the fog had lifted and the day seemed brighter, although the overcast sky made them feel more drunk than they were. Stumbling to Frosty Queen, Edward saddled up and kicked her, startling the horse. She tugged at her reins that were still tied to the post and whinnied as Gavin laughed.

"Shush," Edward chuckled as a few people stared at them but returned to their business when they caught Edward looking back.

"I've got it, I've got it," Gavin slurred as he pulled a knife out. He cut the reins and threw the broken strands up to his friend.

"That was expensive," Edward burped as Gavin laughed. Gavin put his knife away and walked toward his friend. Edward looked down at him and reached down.

"We'll be the ones that end this, and I'll buy you another drink when we get home." Edward said seriously as Gavin nodded.

"I'll meet ya right here," Gavin replied, shaking his friend's hand. "Godspeed," Gavin smirked before smacking Frosty Queen on the haunch causing her speed off in a gallop. He laughed as Edward struggled to stay in the saddle and gain control of his horse.

Chapter 3

Edward sat on Frosty Queen's back, his heart pounding in his ears. He rubbed his temples as the early sun blinded him. His mother stood in the doorway, and his sister and brother stood in front of his horse. Edward meekly climbed down as his sister charged and hugged him. "Don't go, don't go," she whimpered.

"Lily, it will only be a little while," Edward said calmly as Will ran over and hugged the two of them. Edward tried remaining calm and held his tears in as he let his sister and brother go. He looked at his house and watched Andrew step out from behind his mother and slowly walk over.

"Stay safe," Andrew said, calmly holding his hand out. Edward shook his brother's hand sadly. Then Andrew grabbed him by the back of the neck and pulled him into a hug. "I swear to God, if you end up dead, I'll bring you back myself to kill you again," he said.

"Keep the Germans off Frosty Queen's tail and we'll march on," Edward laughed.

Andrew pulled back, pressed his forehead to his brother's and stared at him dead in the eyes. "God guide you, Andrew."

"And you as well." Edward looked up past his brother to his mother and made his way over with Lily following behind him. He hugged her without saying a word.

"Edward, do not say anything of returning home soon, or that you'll come back the same. Because we both know that isn't true. Your father said that to me and never returned. Your brother said that to me and he isn't the same as he was when he left," she spoke calmly, no tears were shed as she hugged her second oldest child.

Edward knelt down next to Will and looked him in the eyes. "You're the man of the house now, William. You keep mommy and Lily safe till Andrew and I come home," he said as William saluted him. Edward laughed and respectfully returned the salute. Then he kissed his family one last time and made his way back to Frosty Queen. "You ready, girl?" he whispered in his horse's ear as she gave a short grunt. He smiled, kissed her cheek, and then saddled up.

He looked over his shoulder as he dug his heels into Frosty Queen's side, making his way to the town square one final time. Andrew walked with his brother neither spoke; neither had anything left to say for fear they would leave it with each other forever. The stress of the day was just starting to settle in. When the square came into view, Edward felt his stomach turning. The town was full of familiar faces, men of all ages. He jumped down from Frosty Queen and grabbed her reins.

"This is where I leave you," Andrew sighed as Edward nodded calmly. Edward reached out first. Andrew shook his head and saluted his brother; both were in uniform and prepared for war. Edward saluted back, his fingers locked tight and palm facing forward. "I'll see you when it's over."

"You take the Germans in the sky, I'll take the Germans on the ground," Edward nodded as Andrew chuckled. Edward caught the glimpse of Gavin who was talking with a group of men in the same uniform as him, and decided not to say goodbye to his friend, knowing their farewell was with the drinks.

"Glad to see you show up, lad," Lieutenant Gyles stated as Edward walked toward his officer in charge.

"Sorry, sir," Edward said sheepishly as the rest of new recruits looked at him oddly.

"Well, let's not hope you're late on the battlefield," Lieutenant Gyles snapped as Edward looked at his feet.

"Y-yes, sir." He knew not to say anything else, and refused to make eye contact for fear of getting more chastised.

"Eyes up, when I'm speaking to you lad," Lieutenant Gyles ordered. Edward obeyed and slowly made eye contact. The Lieutenant looked at Edward seriously and silently before turning away. "You are all my responsibility now, you will follow orders and you follow them the first time," he shouted over the other groups in the square. The small group of seven men stood lined up. "Do I make myself clear?"

"Yes, sir," all seven men said simultaneously.

"Good, now gather the horses and rest of the supplies," Lieutenant Gyles ordered before walking over to his horse.

Edward made his way to Frosty Queen and picked up the rope that coiled around her feet.

Carefully and slowly so he wouldn't frighten his horse.

"Pass me that," one of his new comrades spoke up. Edward looked at the man who pointed at the end of rope. He was young and looked to be a year or two older than Edward. He looked familiar but Edward didn't know everyone in his village. "Cheers," he said as Edward handed him the rope. "Alfred Woodrow," he said extending his hand. Alfred was a foot taller than Edward and his charcoal eyes seemed to show no fear. His black hair cut short and slicked back. His jaw was tight but he gave a sincere smile, "And you might be?"

"Edward Poole," he said shaking Alfred's hand.

"Well, Ed, you watch my back and in return, I'll watch yours," Alfred responded tying the rope to his horse's reins.

"Deal," Edward nodded grabbing two bags of supplies from the pile behind Alfred. "So you live here in town?"

"No, a town over," he answered as Edward tied one of the bags to FrostyQueen's saddle. "I couldn't enlist there."

"Why not?" Edward looked at him oddly, and Alfred responded by shrugging his shoulders as he tied his bags to his horse's saddle.

"They wanted my horse more than me, but wouldn't look at me twice, so I saddled up and came here," he said patting his horse's cheek and kissed the animal on the nose. "I've seen what this war has done to many of my friend's and family, I'm ready to help stop this from continuing."

"We don't know how much longer it will go on anyways." Alfred laughed at Edward's response. The truth of realizing how long this war may

continue on ran through his mind. He thought of
how long he would be away from his home and the
fear started to settle in once more. He didn't realize
that the excitement of signing up would wear off so
fast.

As he tied the second bag onto Frosty
Queen, she turned her head and looked at him. His
horse detected his fear and tried comforting him
with a glance. He smiled and patted her neck. She
whinnied and he laughed before saddling up. He
looked behind him from on top of Frosty Queen and
looked at the line of fourteen horses all tied and
settled ready to be transported to their next location.
Every other horse was saddled and Gyles took to
the front, riding his horse in pace between Edward
and Alfred.

"Wait!" a woman screamed, making
Edward's heart momentarily flutter. The men of the
4th Queens' looked to where the woman called. The
moment of hope quickly left Edward as he spotted a
woman hugging a man in the distance. He looked
away, praying Christine would show up before they
left, but she never came. He despised her for it. She
had left the party with a feeling of detachment, and
not saying goodbye confirmed that.

Gyles trotted ahead as Edward dug his heals
into Frosty Queen's side moving her into a trot, and
soon the rest of the line was keeping the pace. He
peaked over his shoulder as the town grew smaller
and anger filled his veins as he began to despise
himself for ever caring about Christine, knowing
she didn't care if he would return alive or not.

He glimpsed at Alfred who kept his eyes
focused on his horse's neck. Edward wondered
what he was thinking, but kept himself to himself.
The line of horses traveled far and as the town faded

from existence so did Edward's thoughts of
Christine, and his demeanor lifted slightly. He
thought of his family still, and hoped to see them
soon.

"You know you won't be home in a long
time," Gyles spoke quietly as he rode next to Frosty
Queen. Edward hesitantly looked up.

"Sir?"

"Once we get to France that is, it'll be a long
time till you see these lands again."

"I've heard, sir," Edward said. "My
brother... one of the ace fighter pilots."

"Oh your brother is one of those flying
above us. Well next you see him thank him for me,"
Lieutenant Gyles said calmly. "One of those
airplanes saved my life," he said looking out toward
the horizon. Edward looked at him wanting to hear
the story and remained silent knowing it really
wasn't his place to ask. "It was about a year and a
half ago toward the beginning of the war. The
beginning was the hardest part. I saw so many of
my men die. Something I shouldn't be telling you."
Edward felt a pang of fear pulse through his body
but he refused to show it.

"It was the eve of battle, we knew our
chances were going to be slim so we all went to the
pub down the road from our camp. I knew it wasn't
the right thing to do, but we were practically going
to our death. I took my entire platoon to the pub. It
was almost as if we were saying goodbye to the
men who would be losing their lives the following
day. There was one in particular I wanted to keep
my eye on, he was your age," he said seriously. "He
was one of the lucky ones."

"He returned home injury in battle?"
Edward asked.

Lieutenant Gyles shook his head. "He got shot in the heart and died instantly, the rest who died the next day died slowly. I have asked God so many times, why me? How I wish it could have been me." Edward remained silent, not having an answer. "We had a few pints and the entire pub was full with different divisions. I took a booth by myself writing down my thoughts when another soldier, or rather pilot, sat down with me. I closed my journal and looked at the man who joined me. I preferred being alone but clearly the man wanted company. He seemed young to be a pilot and I toasted him. We discussed what was going to happen the next day. Seemed like everyone was going to meet at the war, the Royal Navy, the ace fighters, and my cavalry unit.

He told me to keep an eye on the skies. He told me for every German he takes out of the sky he paints an arrow in the bird. Currently, there was only one arrow. I told him to keep an eye on the enemy above us to give us the time to clear things out of the way on the ground."

Lieutenant Gyles stopped talking as the group slowly trotted onward. Edward looked over his shoulder at Alfred who was talking to his horse. "He'll be the youngest I have ever been in command over," Lieutenant Gyles said. "I'll finish that story later," he looked back at Edward who simply nodded and watched Hannah Gyles pull his horse's reins back toward Alfred. Edward looked ahead, rubbing Frosty Queen's mane.

The next few hours they traveled south. By nightfall they came to a small camp, prepped, and set up. An unsettling feeling of reality came over them as they tied the horses up. Edward made his way to one of the campfires, pulled his journal out and began writing.

"What's that?" Alfred asked pointing to the journal. Edward smirked and closed the small book.

"Just a way to keep track of what's been happening. I've... been writing it since the beginning of the war," he answered, flipping through the pages. "Honestly I don't know why I do it, but it makes me feel better."

"It's your way of coping with what this Great War has given us," Alfred said, sitting next to Edward. "When I sit here and look at Blood Stream, I think maybe this war could have ended sooner, and wonder how it even started."

"Well they say it started with the assassination of the Archduke in Austria-Hungary," Edward answered.

"Ed, I know that, but how did we get involved, what made us want to participate?"

"Well for me, I wanted to get involved when my father died and my brother went into war. I was willing to lie about my age, but my family wouldn't let me." Opening his journal he pulled out a photograph. "That's my family there. My dad is the tall one in the back. He actually did what my brother does. The ace fighter aeroplanes. His plane was shot down over France. They say he died instantly, the plane simply combusted."

"I'm sorry to hear that," Alfred sighed.

"What about you? Why did you sign up?" Alfred seemed to have gotten quiet in that instant. He stared at the fire and handed Edward his photo again. "I'm not holding a gun to your head," Edward said, "you don't have to answer. Looks like we have a good distance to go tomorrow, so I'm

going to turn in," he added. Patting Alfred's
shoulder he made his way toward an empty tent.

Chapter 4

By the time they reached the English Channel, Edward had accepted what was happening with his life. He volunteered to leave. He wanted to fight in the Great War and now he was going to. He knew he no longer could hold onto fear like a nursing blanket. He spat as he climbed down from Frosty Queen, a light hazy rain falling down upon them. "We are going to war soon," he mumbled as Alfred stepped closer to him. "Soon we'll be charging the Germans, pushing their lines back"

"This is the day we'll speak of when we tell our grandchildren, the day the world stood still," Alfred finished Edward's thought. 'The day the world stood still,' the words rang endlessly in Edward's head. The world truly stood still as they watched a ship moving ever so slowly into view, the ship that would take them and their horses to meet with the remaining men of the 4th Queen's Own Hussars.

According to Lieutenant Gyles, it would be another day before they met with the remaining group, but it was always one more day. Edward thought the fear of war prevented him from thinking beyond one day. Tomorrow was a blessing in itself.

He thought quietly to himself as he stared at the ship that crept forward rising and falling on the approaching waves. "France lies beyond those waves, and so does the war."

"We will be in France for a while," Gyles said as Edward looked up to him.

"Keep those bloody bastards at bay."

Everyone laughed.

"The real war, currently resides in Arras. It will be soon enough that they are knocking on the doors of Arras. We are going to win that war first," he said strongly.

"Lieutenant," Edward said quietly standing next to the man. "Will you finish that story?"

"I will," Lieutenant Gyles nodded, wrapping his hands in the reins of his horse looking down at Edward. "But as I said, another day," he announced as he climbed down from his horse. "Gentlemen," he said sternly, looking at the seven men who stood next to the horses. "Make sure the horses are tied up comfortably before finding your quarters."   The men nodded in unison.

"Yes, sir," they all said.

After a few minutes of waiting around, the ship finally docked. Hardly anyone climbed off, and those that did were being helped or carried off by medics. Those that survived their injuries and more than likely would not be returning to the front lines.

"Lucky bastards," Edward heard someone mumbled under their breath. He looked over his shoulder at a man dressed in the uniform of the British army. He seemed to be in his late twenties or early thirties, and his jaw line made him look serious and angry. His sharp grey eyes glanced at Edward, who caught him looking. "What about you?" he barked. "I saw you, you can't act like you weren't giving me your attention," the man sighed as Edward looked back again. "You know it's true, you wouldn't have looked if you didn't agree," he said pointing to the wounded.

"I... looked because your words simply surprise me," Edward said calmly.

"You have no clue what is entailed for you," the man grumbled.

Edward took offense to the man's remark but remained silent. He listened to the man go on about the trenches and what was waiting for them, and he didn't really understand whether the man was talking to him or himself.

A small whistle pipe blew, and Lieutenant Gyles led his horse up the gantry while Edward watched on. "Go on, join your clan," the man said. Edward ignored him and walked Frosty Queen forward. As the horse approached the gantry, she began to huff and whine.

"Come on, girl," Edward sighed, tugging at her reins as the horse pranced about nervously huffing and puffing. "Come on." He fought pulling the weight of muscle.

"Poole!" Lieutenant Gyles barked over the railing. "That horse is scared, you don't force it when it's scared," he continued talking as he walked down the gantry and ripped the reins from Edward's hand. He whispered in Frosty Queen's ear petting her nose until she calmed down. "Now," he said taking a deep breath, "climb up on her." Edward did as he was instructed. "Cover her eyes, like blinders." Edward leaned forward, placing his head on her neck he did what the lieutenant asked.

"Come on girl, nice and slowly," Gyles instructed, tugging lightly on Frosty Queen's reins. The horse slowly crept forward, putting one hoof in front of the other. He took her up the gantry and stopped her when she stood on the deck of the ship. "You can uncover her eyes now."

Edward obeyed, climbed down and took the reins once more. "Thank you," he said nervously as his Lieutenant patted his shoulder before walking away.

"What a horse you have there, a prize to win the war," the man mocked as he stepped on the ship. Edward held his tongue as he tugged on his horse's reins. They followed after Alfred and the horses he guided. The 4th Queen's Own Hussar's gathered the horses in the stern of the ship. The ship rocked in port, the strong waves from the channel already making Edward's stomach unsteady as he tied Frosty Queen to the railing.

"We're going," Alfred said, his voice carrying uncertainty.

"Yes, Alf, we're going. And I told you, you watch my back I watch yours."

"I was the one who told you that." Edward nodded as he and Alfred walked from the horses. They quickly made their way down below deck and found their quarters. "You know what I don't understand? We'll be making landfall in France by sundown, so why do we have quarters?"

"To make you feel relaxed before they send you to hell," the man said, standing in the doorway. "I don't want to share a room with you as much as you do," he smirked at Edward, who threw his bag on the bed.

"Alfred Woodrow," Alfred smiled offering the man his hand. "We're all fighting the same war for the same reason," he smiled as the man shook his hand.

"Thomas Wellings," the man said sternly. Edward rummaged through his bag and pulled his notebook out. "And you might be?" Thomas looked at Edward who glanced up from his journal.

"Um… Edward Poole," he answered carefully before returning to his journal. The room became silent and an awkward presence surrounded everyone as they all took seats on the beds. Edward wrote quietly thoughts no longer consumed and driven by fear. He wrote about what he thought awaited for him. Then, he flipped through his journal to his first entry and noted how drastically in two years his journal changed. He missed his father and felt closer to him more than ever, even after death.

"I'm going for a walk," Alfred broke the silence as Edward looked up from his journal. He nodded and returned to writing and Alfred nodded awkwardly before walking out of the room leaving Edward with Tom.

"How old are you?" Tom asked, leaning on his knees as he sat at the edge of his bed. Edward looked up from his journal, but remained silent. "A simple question, sixteen? Seventeen?"

"I didn't lie about my age, I'm eighteen," he said sarcastically.

"I don't understand," said Tom, "Why anyone in their God given lives would want to volunteer and lie about their age to go into this hell hole?"

"They want to serve Crown and Country?"

"That's the question why? After what you see out there, you'll understand. I wanted to…"

"You were a deserter?"

"Almost," Tom snapped. "But this is war. The Great War, and all it has left is devastation, and families separated sometimes never to be seen again." Edward tucked his journal back in his bag, Tom's words ringing in his ears.

"My father never came home. We know he died. But he may have been buried in no man's land or he wasn't even recovered. They saw my father's plane go down so they know." Tom became quiet for the first time. Since meeting Edward, he had nothing to say. "I... I think I'm going to meet up with Alf," Edward finished by standing and making his way out of the room.

He walked down the hall rocking as the ship crossed the channel. He felt sicker the further down the hall he walked. He climbed the stairs to the main deck and leaned on the rail, staring at the waves that crashed into the ship rocking it back and forth his skin turning a pale color.

"You alright there?" Alfred laughed walking over to his friend. Edward spit out at the salty water and nodded. "Keep an eye on the horizon not the water," he added as Edward listened and lifted his head. The two leaned on the railing for a while.

"What made you enlist?" Edward finally said as Alfred looked at him.

"Pardon?"

"For the war, what made you enlist, Alf?" Edward asked still looking at the horizon trying to distract himself from the rough waves.

"Oh, well... my brothers, actually," he said nervously. "I... I have three older brothers, each out in the war. Two of them are sailors in the Royal Navy."

"And the third?" Edward asked.

Alfred shrugged. "I honestly don't know. We all expect the worst. He was being sent to Ypres with the British Army," he answered. "He sent letters from the trenches. From what I read they are the worst part of this war, miles of trenches that need to be dug out every night. Every night they spend their time digging out new sections with explosions going on throughout the night." Edward stood quietly listening to his friend. When Alfred finally finished, the two fell silent.

"So why did you enlist, Alf?" Edward returned to his original question.

"Why did you sign up?" Alfred countered.

"I wanted to fight for my country the same way my father died serving his and my brother does now by flying above the battles. I want to be a hero that has a name carved into history, even if my name is only known to my family. Now why did you enlist?"

"Because I was tired of being scared," Alfred finally spoke up. "I was scared the German's would come to my village and slaughter everyone. I enlisted to protect my family and friends and join my brother's on the battlefield."

"How old are you, Alf?" Alfred became silent and smiled a little as Edward looked at him out of the corner of his eye. "I know you aren't eighteen."

"I a-"

"Because!" Edward cut him off, "because Lieutenant Gyles made one mistake and told me you were the youngest soldier he was going to be looking out for. I just turned eighteen a few days ago, signed up the day after my eighteenth birthday, so unless we share the same birthday, you are not eighteen."

"Alright, yes I lied about my age. I'm really sixteen, but I'm not the only one doing so, last year a twelve-year-old from where I live signed up, fought in the Battle of the Somme, and is still fighting, so why is it a big deal? I'm two years younger than the required age and I'm the best rider north of London," Alfred said cockily.

"Fine," Edward smirked, "when we get some free time, Frosty Queen and I versus you and Blood Stream," he laughed offering Alfred his hand.

"Deal!" Alfred laughed shaking his hand. The two became quiet once more, Edward focusing on the horizon and trying to settle his nauseous feeling by thinking of dry land while Alfred leaned on the rail staring at the waves below. They remained in silent company for a few minutes. "I'm scared," Alfred whispered trying to force a laugh out.

"I know. In a way, I am too," Edward said. "But this is what I had been waiting to do, when we left home yesterday, the fear was the strongest and it remained with me until the moment I got Frosty Queen on the ship. Honestly Alf, it's all right to be afraid. Nothing we know for certain will lead for our time onward. But what we do know is tomorrow is on the way, and we live for that. For as long as we stand, so do our homes," Edward said without taking his gaze from the horizon.

Chapter 5

14 March, 1917

We arrived in camp several hours ago. According to Lieutenant Gyles, we're about a thirty-minute walk to the city of Arras. Tonight was one hell of a night. I learned a few things from my friends. George, whom I met on arrival, told Alf and I some interesting stories. But I'm getting ahead of myself. After the seven of us made it to camp, we started settling in. Some got to know the ones who we'd be fighting with, listening to what they had to say on the war. Others like myself immediately settled in.

That is until Lieutenant Gyles pulled me aside. We discussed what the next few weeks would entail. I thought he was joking at first, but he wants Alf and I to take orders solely from him. Although I don't think we can do that on technicalities of only being troopers. If an order comes from a commanding officer, we must do it. But I humored him and agreed to his terms. I guess it brought a peace to his mind. When I left his lodging and made my way back to where Alf and I were camped, I found Alf talking to George. I was thrown off for a second when George invited us to the city for some drinks. I mean we are at bloody war and he's inviting us to drinks. But when I noticed a good number of our company walking away from the camp, I assumed we all had the night off so I agreed and joined them. When we reached Arras, it was half eight.

The town was nearly quiet; the other buildings were all dark except for the pubs. George took Alf and I to his favorite, called Crème de la Crème. I wish I was making that name up, but I'm not. The place was stuffed to the rafters with people. When we first entered I was a bit overwhelmed with the noise and the heat, but it was a welcoming feeling compared to the dropping temperature of night. I went off with Alf to find a spot where the three of us could sit while George got the drinks at the bar.

While we waited, Alf and I talked about our families back home. I didn't realize how much I'd miss home until I got here. There was a small ping of homesickness when I left, but when I woke this morning, I felt like a wreck. Anyway, Alf told me he was the middle child of seven and that when he signed up his mum wasn't too pleased. I could understand her dissatisfaction completely. He was sixteen. Technically, I'm still too young for this war but what's the difference between eighteen and nineteen, really? But I couldn't help but laugh when Alf told me that his mother walloped him and pushed him against the wall yelling. Again, I can understand her annoyance.

Then George returned with the drinks. I looked at my pocket watch, realizing we only had about an hour before we needed to make our way back to the camp. George told me not to worry too much about it. We sat for a good twenty minutes talking about what we did before the war. I couldn't say much considering I was fifteen and working on my farm when the war broke out.

Since I was the one facing the door, I could see every person coming and going. I didn't pay much attention until this pretty brunette walked in. I excused myself from the table and made my way over. Her name was Adeline and she was selling poppies. I bought her a beer instead. She gave me a one of her poppies. We talked for only a few minutes. Her English was broken and stuck to speaking French, which I could barely understand. George came over and started speaking to her in French. I feel he may have said something about me since she looked at me and began to giggle. She left her half-drunk beer on the bar and when George brought me back to the table, we resumed our conversation. Although I was listening, I couldn't stop thinking about her. Her voice was so angelic and her eyes were as blue as topaz. I wanted to get to know her. I don't understand what came over me. No woman had ever made me this awkward.

By 21:10 we'd finished our drinks and were making our way back to camp. When I looked at my pocket watch, I noticed we only had twenty minutes to get back. We had a curfew and were supposed to stick to it religiously. I started to get worried knowing we had a thirty-minute walk.

George remembered a "shortcut" that was in no way a shortcut back to camp. I asked George what made him get into the war. He told us that he signed up at the beginning of the war at the age of twenty-two. Alf asked him what living through the first year was like. George just told us stories the entire walk back. He also shared what it was like to experience the great Christmas Truce of 1914. I reminded myself to write down the details in a letter to Gavin. I remember the day the papers published the photos from the Truce. It gave us a different feel of the war. We were killing other Christians. They weren't animals, but men. I remember talking to Gavin and discussing our concerns, but that still didn't extinguish the feeling of wanting to fight for crown and country.

I wonder how Gavin is doing. I should write my letter soon before, God forbid, anything happens. He's a good friend of mine. I'd consider him my closest pal to be honest, practically a brother.

Where was I? Oh right, George told his stories to Alf and I as we walked into the camp quarter till eleven. The camp was quiet. We thought we could make it to our tents without getting caught. But there he was, Lieutenant Gyles standing right outside his tent, arms folded looking stern as ever.

"Were you not instructed to be back at 22:30?" His question wasn't direct to anyone. We all looked at our feet like little children being scolded. I felt like I was in primary school all over again, and made the mistake of chuckling at that very moment. It made him madder. We tried telling him the reason why we were late was that George's shortcut was far from a shortcut. He didn't want to hear our protests. And now we have to scrub all the horses after training tomorrow. He dismissed us and we returned to our tents.

Alf fell asleep maybe ten minutes ago. I can't sleep. I'll try again in a little while. I do understand why I enlisted; the feeling is stronger now than ever as I write this. But something tells me I was in the wrong. I know I'm not and I am ready to stand up for every right my country stands for. We will fight with our allies soon and I intend to be ready, whatever training has in store for me.

- Trooper Edward Jacob Poole

Chapter 6

Dawn had yet to come when Edward was woken. He gasped and panted as George stood over him. "Take a deep breath," George laughed before shaking Alfred awake who reacted the same way Edward had moments before. Both boys groggily climbed from their cots and exited their tent following close behind George. The camp was quiet, the sun was an hour away from rising.

"What are we doing?" Alfred yawned, while George remained silent. They walked toward the horses and the two watched as George untied what they assumed to be his horse.

"What are you waiting on, grab your horse," George ordered as Edward and Alfred looked at each other. "That is an order."

"And we should trust you?" Edward whispered.

"You were the one who got us in trouble for returning to camp late," Alfred but in.

"If you two don't get your horses, you'll be cleaning more than the horses when training is done today," George threatened as Edward yawned.

"You're a trumpeter…"

"Yes, I am, which last I checked is higher than your rank, so get your horse," George whispered as Edward sighed. He made his way to Frosty Queen and contemplated listening to George or defying him, which made for quite the dilemma. As they mounted their horses Edward's thoughts cleared, and he looked at the tent in which Lieutenant Gyles would be sleeping. "Follow." George kicked his own horse and took off toward Arras.

"Stay close," he whispered to Alfred who nodded, and the two took off following behind George's horse. The cold morning would chill any man to the bone but Edward loved the chill. In the moments of that morning, the ride to wherever they were going seemed to make him forget about the world's current state. He forgot of the war and he felt like he was once again home on his little farm riding home from a long day, forgetting the world and focusing only on himself. He closed his eyes, knowing Frosty Queen would lead. He thought of his brother William and sister Lily and his mother waiting in the door frame. He saw his brother Andrew laughing as he walked by him toward their home. He dreamed of the day the war would end and prayed the day would be soon.

The sun was rising in his daydream and as it rose, he saw the chocolate haired beauty with the name of Adeline. She was just as much an angel in his dreams than she was in real life.

"Edward!" George shouted as he opened his eyes and quickly pulled back on Frosty Queen's reins pulling her to a rough stop. She slid on the dew-laced grass, almost colliding with George's horse.

"That is the sloppiest stop I have ever seen!" Lieutenant Gyles shouted as Edward looked over his shoulder at his approaching Lieutenant.

"Yes, sir," Edward mumbled, somewhat ashamed of himself for being caught daydreaming. "I was..."

"No excuses. You talk less and listen more." Edward nodded shamefully.

"Excuse me, sir?" Alfred spoke up.

"Am I talking to you, Woodrow?" Gyles barked, causing the sixteen-year-old to jump.

"No, no, sir," he fumbled on his own words as Lieutenant Gyles returned his attention to Edward.

"Now do you know what you did wrong?"

"I let my guard down, sir," Edward said quietly.

"I can't hear, you did what now?"

"I... I let my guard down, sir."

"And what happens when we let our guard down? Williams?"

"You get struck by a bullet or shrapnel sir," George said, glaring at Edward seriously. The group of four suddenly became quiet. Gyles looked up at the stars and back at his men. "Now, why are we out an hour before the rest of the company arrives?"

"To be prepared for what lies beyond the camp, sir?" Alfred spoke up.

"The beginning of our punishment, sir," George sighed, regretting staying twenty past the hour, but Lieutenant Gyles simply shook his head.

"May I ask why, sir?" Edward spoke up as the older man nodded and looked at them.

"Nothing brings a unit closer than comradely. We train together, we learn each other's strengths and weaknesses. But you three, there is a reason I had George take you two to the pub last night. A year ago, I swore to myself and I swore to God, that during this war, if I were to get any man under the age of twenty I would do everything in my power to make sure they see it through this war. I would train them with my best men, and let them learn from myself personally." Edward looked at his Lieutenant and saw a pain in his eyes, a pain as no man should ever need to carry. "This war has taken much from us all."

"I signed up with my friends," George said as Alfred and Edward looked at him. "Seven of us joined, and six have already died. I buried each of them myself."

"Many did as George had done, they signed with their friends seeking fame, or something else. I stand before you to tell you to put your stubborn thoughts aside and take my orders, my orders that may just keep you alive to see beyond tomorrow, because not knowing the day after tomorrow is a scary vision. A vision I no longer can see. Your childhood innocence is the most important thing in this world, hold onto it and don't let it go," Lieutenant Gyles said calmly. His strong harsh exterior seemed to melt before their eyes, and a genuine God-fearing man stood before them.

"Now, take to the course, Williams, show them," he ordered as George kicked his horse taking to the course. Alfred and Edward sat on watching George and his horse jump over strands of barbed wire and pits of mud and small trenches. They watched him draw his sword and stab a bag of hay. After jumping a stream, he sheathed his sword and pulled a small pistol out before shooting the last hay bag and then trotting his horse back to the group. "You think you two can do that?"

"Aye, sir," Edward answered first. "You ready to show me what Blood Stream can do?" Edward taunted as Alfred smirked.

"Come on," he instructed Frosty Queen, giving her sides a little tap with his heels. She took to an immediate trot with Blood Stream close behind. She remained ahead, jumping over the barbed wire fine and trotting through mud and jumping the trenches. Edward drew his sword, a wide smile on his face, but missed his target and his smile quickly faded.

Blood Stream came up from his left side passing him and Alfred laughed. "Faster!" Edward commanded, nudging Frosty Queen as she raced to a gallop, surpassing Blood Stream. As the stream approached, Edward struggled to switch from sword to pistol. When his sword was sheathed and the pistol in his hand, he prepped Frosty Queen to jump the stream, rising off the saddle and leaning forward. Edward didn't expect a loud frightening whinny to come from his horse. She skated across the wet grass trying to stop as Edward flew from the saddle flipping over her head and landing on his shoulder in the stream.

Edward surfaced soaking wet and coughing on fresh water.

"You all right?" Alfred asked climbing down from Blood Stream.

Edward sat in the creek holding his shoulder. "I'm fine," he groaned slowly standing.

"Everything..."

"I'm fine," Edward said again as Lieutenant Gyles and George approached.

Frosty Queen pranced about frightened and George grabbed her reins. Edward climbed out of the stream and took his horse's reins from George.

Edward stared in his horse's chocolate eye almost studying her. "I don't know what has gotten into you."

"If she can't jump that creek..."

"She can," Edward protested. "I know she can."

"Some horses aren't fit for war," Lieutenant Gyles stated as Edward rubbed her under her chin.

"She will be," Edward replied, looking at his horse and ignoring the fact he was completely soaked.

"Then do it again."

At Lieutenant Gyles orders, Edward climbed back onto Frosty Queen's back. He pulled her reins in the direction of the start of the course.

"This time worry about completing the actual track," Gyles instructed.

Edward dug his heels into his horse's sides. Slowly, he took some of her mane and tangled his right hand within it before grabbing the reins again. She let out a soft grunt; one Edward was actually hoping to hear. He ignored the dummy statues he was supposed to practicing on and focused on the jump that was fast approaching.

"Come on girl," he whispered leaning closer to her. She started to pick up her pace and Edward began smiling, but his smile soon faded when he heard her whinny and skate to a stop once more. The entire group let out a simultaneous sigh as Edward climbed down from his horse disappointed. By this time the rest of the 4th Queen's Own Hussar's were approaching on their horses.

"Training before the rest of the battalion again, Gyles?" a man walked over to the small group.

"Yes, sir, can never be too careful, especially with new blood," Gyles said strictly saluting the man who approached.

The man took his cap off and placed it under his arm, Edward glanced at the man's shoulder, seeing it was decorated with three small diamonds. Edward could tell this man was much higher ranked than their Lieutenant.

"Captain Hemsworth," George spoke up.

"Why am I not surprise you're apart of this, probably getting into more trouble," Hemsworth sighed, pointing at George. His hazel eyes studied the trumpeter before returning to Edward. The man ran his hand through his sandy brown hair and looked at Alfred. "More boys, to die for a cause they don't know," Captain Hemsworth said calmly as Alfred glanced at Edward, but Edward never moved or said a word. "Very well, you three, in the trenches, you'll be working on 'duties of the front,'" Hemsworth said making air quotes.

Edward, Alfred, and George followed close behind Hemsworth and made their way into a partially dug trench. For the next several hours, the boys took shots at dummies practicing their sniping, taking cover in the trench, and most importantly, learning all the tactics of trench warfare.

An hour before five, Captain Hemsworth discussed his thoughts with his small group of four or five lieutenants. They periodically glanced at the men who stood still holding their reins of their horses. Edward focused his eyes on a small farmhouse in the distance letting his mind wander thinking of home.

"Poole," Hemsworth spoke from the group, as Edward looked up fuzzy from his daydreaming. "Come here, Poole!" Edward awkwardly handed

Alfred FrostyQueen's reins and briskly walked to the group of superiors. Hemsworth looked at him from head to toe, studying him. Edward felt an uncomfortable judgment fall upon him. "Ride the course," Hemsworth ordered.

"Sir?"

"You will refer to me as Captain Hemsworth, or simply captain," the man snapped as Edward nodded awkwardly. "Now, ride the course."

"Si- I mean, captain, Frosty Queen isn't..."

"Did I ask you to give me an explanation? Now get on your horse and ride the course."

"Y-yes, captain," Edward ran back to the line. He quickly jumped on Frosty Queen and looked down at Alfred who looked as worried as Edward felt. "Come on girl," he whispered running his hand through her mane, "it's just you and me, no need to be scared." He trotted her to the start and looked at Captain Hemsworth and then Lieutenant Gyles, who nodded giving him the okay to start. Edward could see the uneasiness on his face, too.

He started Frosty Queen into a trot, taking her up and down the small mounds in the course. Ignoring the people watching, he gently jumped her over the trench he had been practicing all day in. Drawing his sword, he stabbed the dummy and turned the horse toward the creek that finished the course.

He quickly sheathed his sword and remembered getting her onto ship a day ago. Leaning forward, Edward cupped his hands on either side of Frosty Queen's eyes making her only see straight ahead. He closed his eyes as she approached the creek and suddenly felt weightless. He couldn't believe she was leaping.

"Yes!" Alfred screamed from the line, causing Edward to smile until Frosty Queen landed. His chest slammed into the pommel of the saddle and the wind was forced from his body causing him to double over and fall from the saddle landing on his back. "No!" Alfred could be heard taking his cheering back.

"Woodrow!" Captain Hemsworth shouted, silencing the young soldier. Edward lay in the grass trying to get the air back in his lungs as Frosty Queen walked over. She leaned down, sniffing his face, before licking at his hair.

When Frosty Queen was pulled off, he noticed Hemsworth's group looking down at him.

"You hurt, boy?" Hemsworth asked.

Edward shook his head.

"Then why are you still laying down playing with your horse?" the captain shouted and Edward felt small once again. Lieutenant Gyles offered him his hand and helped him up. "When we return to camp, you'll be bathing the horses."

"He, Williams, and Woodrow are already doing that Captain," Lieutenant Gyles said as Hemsworth looked at Edward.

"Well now, it is just Poole cleaning the horses," Hemsworth said turning from them.

"Yes, Captain," Edward said strongly and saluted. Captain Hemsworth stopped and turned to Gyles and then Edward who still stood in the saluted position.

"Are you mocking me, Poole?"

"No, Captain," he shouted, still saluting. "Just serving the way I know, Captain," Edward said trying to suppress the frustration he was feeling. Hemsworth saluted Edward though, to his surprise. He was in a way showing the captain attitude, but earned respect he thought he would not get.

"Oh and Poole, get your horse blinders," Hemsworth said sternly before walking away. The Lieutenants left and gathered their groups.

"What were you thinking?" Gyles whispered not approvingly as Edward felt that small feeling again.

"I... I don't know, sir," he said calmly as Alfred and George joined them. "Looks like you two are off horse duty today, our friend here is doing the cleaning by himself."

"But-" Alfred went to protest, but George slammed the back of his hand on Alfred's chest to shut him up.

"Gather the horses," Gyles instructed as the three took to their horses and made their way back to camp. When they arrived, the horses of the 4th Queen's Own Hussars lined up and half the camp seemed empty. Edward assumed the lads had gone into town to the pub. "Add the horses, and Edward get to work. Alfred, George, you two have the night off," Gyles sighed as they lined their horses with the others.

"Maybe we'll see you at the pub afterwards?" Alfred said as Edward forced a smile.

"Don't drink too much, Alf," Edward joked as the sixteen-year-old laughed.

George and Alfred began walking away with Lieutenant Gyles. "Oh, Lieutenant," Edward said pulling a folded letter out of his pocket. "Can you send this home for me?" he asked holding out the letter he wrote to his family before bed the night before. Lieutenant Gyles nodded and took the letter before walking away.

Chapter 7

Three weeks had passed since Edward's first
day in the camp. Many days of training on
horseback and in trenches. A few nights at the pub,
and a few nights sleeping early. Alfred woke him
early on the first day they had a break.

"What time is it?" Edward groaned as
Alfred shone his torch in his face. "Alf," he sighed
shoving the torch away.

"You said you'd race Blood Stream and I,"
Alfred smirked as Edward sat up rubbing his eyes.
A loom of dread hovered over him this morning, but
he tried to not think so much of war and doom.
Pulling himself from his slumber he quickly
changed into his uniform and followed Alfred out of
the tent. Alfred began laughing as he untied Blood
Stream while Edward shushed him.

"Alf, its early, most of the company is
sleeping," Edward said in a quiet tone. He untied
Frosty Queen and pulled her from the other horses.

"Edward," Lieutenant Gyles called from his
tent, causing both Alfred and Edward to freeze.
Slowly, Gyles walked to the two. Edward felt a
sinking a feeling in his gut. When he caught sight of
his Lieutenant, he noticed a small box in his hand.

"This arrived for you this morning," he said. Edward noticed the package wrap had been removed and suspected that whatever the contents were had been partially removed. "Keep it close, and keep it secret," he said carefully handing him the box. "This is one thing that really shouldn't be here, but I don't see the harm," he said.

Edward opened the package and pulled out a small rectangular-looking black box with a window in the middle. He knew what the little box was, a vest pocket Kodak. Edward pulled the letter from the box and began reading while Gyles walked away.

"It's from my mother," Edward spoke up before Alfred could ask. "Turns out my friend Gavin owns one, his mother sent him one a few weeks back. So I guess my mother thought I'd want one," he laughed reading and rereading the letter with a small smile. He tucked the carbon paper and the VPK in his chest pocket. "You ready for a race?" he smirked at Alfred before climbing onto Frosty Queen. "First to Arras wins?" he smiled as Alfred climbed onto Blood Stream. "Loser buys breakfast?"

"You're on," Alfred smiled, kicking Blood Stream and taking off into a gallop.

"Hey!" Edward shouted as Frosty Queen galloped toward Blood Stream. When they broke through the woods and into the open fields Blood Stream was only a few feet ahead of Frosty Queen. Edward caught Alfred glance over his shoulder, a wide smile on his face. "Pay attention!" Edward yelled kicking Frosty Queen again and leaning forward. Frosty Queen was closing the gap and the town of Assar was coming into view. "Come on girl," Edward whispered as the two horses galloped into town Blood Stream only a few meters ahead.

"I won," Alfred gloated as the two boys stopped their horses.

"Very well, you won, so let's get a photo of the winner," Edward smiled, pulling his VPK out. Placing a piece of carbon paper in the slot he extended the front window and turned the dial to adjust it for the light of the sun.

"Wait," Alfred said, grabbing Frosty Queen's reins. "She deserves to be in the picture as well," he smiled standing between both horses.

Edward placed the VPK to his stomach as he looked at the mirror in the top of the opening making sure both animals and Alfred could be seen. Clicking down on the button, he snapped the first shot of many to follow. He looked up at a grinning Alfred and laughed before he noticed Adeline walking away from the pub, her basket of poppies hanging on her arm.

"I'll be right back," Edward said, walking past Alfred who looked over his shoulder to where Edward was heading. "Madam," Edward called out as Adeline turned to see who called her, her hair twirling as she did so. "Bonjour," he smiled.

"Bonjour, comment allez-vous?" she smiled back.

"I'm good, and yourself?"

"Good," her cheeks were a soft pink in the pale glow of the street lamps.

"Have you eaten? Would you like to join my friend and I?" he asked pointing to Alfred who stood awkwardly with two horses in his hands.

"Pardon?" she shook her head quizzically.

"Um... eat, food?" he said slowly making a motion toward his mouth and rubbing his stomach.

"Déjeuner?" she clapped her hands in excitement.

"Oui, déjeuner, oui," he nodded as her smile fell short a little.

"No, I… um… already," she said trying to speak in English for him.

"Oh," he sighed.

"But, some other time?" She said easily. Edward clenched his jaw as he politely nodded.

"Are you sure, you're not too busy?" He felt pushy, a feeling he didn't like, but something about this girl made his head spin.

"Oui," she giggled, "I'm… how you say, positive," she giggled again. "I really must be going," she said politely. "It was, um, very nice to see you again."

"And you as well," he sighed as she started to walk away.

"Well that wasn't awkward," Alfred laughed, walking over to him as he glared at his friend. "Come on, lets get some food. I'm starving," he added as Edward took Frosty Queen's reins. He tied her to a post near the door and followed in after Alfred.

The pub wasn't as busy as the last time they had been there, but men in uniforms still littered the small space. The two boys took a seat in the back far from the others who had gathered. They ordered a simple breakfast and sat in silence waiting, Alfred rested his head on the wall, closing his eyes briefly. "Could you imagine the world being this bad?" He asked, opening one eye and looking at Edward who had a concerning look on his face.

"Honestly, I could, the tension has been there for years," Edward answered, "but Alf, we're the wall against evil, we're the ones saving our lands."

"We are the ones riding our horses into slaughter," Alfred sighed as Edward felt a darkness fall on him. When he heard Alfred's words he saw the fear in his friend for the first time. Not the fear of not knowing what's coming, not the fear of speaking up to him or others, not the fear of even taking someone else's life, but the fear of having his life taken. Edward didn't know what to say. He felt a knot stuck in his throat, and he felt the fear he saw in Alfred's eyes.

"We'll make it out, together, with our horses"

"And how are you so sure?"

"I'm..." Edward sighed as their breakfasts were placed before them, "thank you," he said, looking at the woman who dropped off the hot meals. "I'm not sure, but what I am sure about is this hot meal is well waited for," he said trying to smile but Alfred wouldn't give it to him. "Blood Stream is a good horse, he'll keep you moving fast and sharply," Edward smirked before taking a bite from his bacon.

"Look, I don't want to talk much about this, but I want to feel somewhat secure."

"Alf, you're in good hands with Lieutenant Gyles, myself, and George," Edward laughed as Alfred smirked a little, trying to make an effort to smile.

"It's not about my well being, it's about Blood Stream... and I've heard rumors that rider-less horses get resold."

"Don't think like that," Edward sighed placing the bacon down.

"It's kind of hard not to when we're getting closer every day. I sometimes lie in bed in the middle of the night wondering where Blood Stream would end up if I... fell," he mumbled.

"Alf, I promise you, I won't let you fall."

"I expect you to keep that promise," Alfred said finally smiling as Edward chuckled. But he quickly lost the smile and was defeated by his thoughts once more. "Look, all I want to ask is, God forbid something happens, you'll... take care of Blood Stream for me, and write my sister and parents?"

Edward sat in shock that his friend was even asking of him something so serious and he felt a massive weight fall upon his shoulders. The shock settled in and Alfred stared at him making the weight even heavier. The fear Edward saw in Alfred's eyes changed to something more concerning, but he let out a long sigh to let the stress of the question leave him.

"I promise, if... if God forbid, something were to happen to you and you fell, then I'll take care of Blood Stream," Edward said as Alfred sighed and leaned back as if one weight of many had been taken from him.

"And I promise the same if something were to happen to you. Then, Frosty Queen would be in good hands."

"Thanks Alf, I know you mean well," Edward said slowly trying to not let the concern get to him. He took another bite from his bacon, the salt taste turning sour in his mouth and sat contemplating as if something else was eating at his thoughts. Maybe it was something or maybe it was nothing. He barely listened to Alfred who had tried changing the subject to a more lively conversation, he only answered when he assumed his friend wanted a response. He couldn't help but feel a presence of something greater and wondered if Alfred felt it too. He assumed he did since he brought up the subject of either of them dying, but his thoughts were shattered on why.

The two finished their breakfast not long after, or what seemed like a short time to Edward. After gathering their things they left in silence, collected their horses in silence, and road back to camp in silence. As they arrived, they noticed the camp a bit frenzied.

"Where the hell have you two been?" George whispered as Edward and Alfred climbed off their horses.

"We went to get breakfast. What... what's going on?"

"We're moving camp eastward," George answered Edward's question with a solid seriousness and readiness. "We're going to just outside the city. We're going to make the front," he finished and Edward stood frozen as if he got punched in the stomach and would vomit his breakfast right then and there. He began wondering if he was even ready. This was that feeling he felt before, the feeling of not knowing where the future would take him, not knowing what lay around the bend. This was the dreaded weight of knowing he was about to step into war.

Chapter 8

Edward helped break the camp down, a small smile on his face knowing this was the moment he had been waiting for. His mind seemed jammed with what would wait for him at the front. Slowly he packed, thinking to himself how he was going to be the hero in the sight of every man, woman, and child back home. He paused as he thought of home. He thought of his family warm in their beds, and then he thought of his brother flying somewhere over France. His thoughts drifted a little more, letting him wonder if Gavin was having the same adventures as he was or what a tank engineer would be doing.

"Edward," Alfred spoke up. "You all right? I've been calling you for a few minutes now." Edward nodded silently and smiled a little.

"I'm fine, Alf, just thinking of friends and family out in the war, wondering what they're doing," Alfred handed an end of the flattened tent, wanting him to help him fold it.

"Well keep your mind from drifting, you'll stay alive longer," George said walking past them.

When the camp was fully packed up, the horses were saddled and ready, the men of the 4th

Queen's Own Hussars saddled their horses and moved eastward. The last thing to run through Edward's mind was Adeline; he could see her face as clear as day. Her smile sent butterflies fluttering around his stomach and made him feel happy. He barely knew this girl, and he was head over heels for her.

"Now what are you thinking about?" Alfred asked, trotting Blood Stream up next to Frosty Queen.

"Nothing," Edward chuckled as they kept the pace with the company. The two became quiet. "This is it, Alf," Edward broke the silence between them again. Alfred looked at his friend with a small smile. "How long's it been?"

"Since what? Arriving? Easily a month?" Alfred thought back.

"Has it? Maybe... but could we be ready?"

"No, one's ready," George spoke up as he slowed his horse to ride with Edward and Alfred. "What is coming to us, what we are going into, no matter what training has done for you, truly no one is ready."

Edward fell silent, not knowing how to respond to what George has said.   "This war is fought from the trenches no side advancing no side gaining."

"That's not true, the Battle of the Somme..."

"The beginning of that battle we lost sixty five thousand, and that's just of our men," George interrupted Alfred, who became just as quiet as Edward. "A week straight we dropped shells on the Germans thinking that would destroy their machine guns and when they let our lads run out of the trenches they were gunned down."

"But we did win in the end," Alfred spoke up again.

"After four months of fighting, sure," George scowled and now we are destined right for the front line in Arras."

"How did we let them get this close?" Edward asked as George looked out to the head of the line. A sea of men and horses traveled in front of them and behind. Edward could tell George had no answer and kicked Frosty Queen to get her to pick up the pace. Pushing his way a few rows, he trotted next to Lieutenant Gyles.

"Stepping into battle, I'm sure the blood is pumping in your veins," Lieutenant Gyles chuckled, obviously trying to make light of the subject. Edward forced a smile as Alfred and George approached. "Clearly, the pals have arrived," Gyles looked to Alfred next to him and George next to Edward. "What seems to be on your minds?"

"How did we let the Germans get so close?"

"When things go wrong, we hold them back in other places," Lieutenant Gyles answered.

"Well of course, but that's not the answer I was looking for. Why our infantry?"

"Arras needs men we are right here. Why not us? We have a plan to take on the Germans and when our task is completed, we can then head south to Cannes or Cambrai."

"Cannes? Cannes is on the other side of the country, far south actually," Edward nearly yelped as Gyles chuckled.

"We don't choose were we go, we have orders, we follow those orders. And currently our orders are taking us to protect Arras, where we will give those Germans a major set back," Gyles smirked as Edward sighed.

The distance to travel from their old camp to the new location just east of the city wasn't too far the sooner they could arrive, the sooner they could help protect the city and those who remained. Not many people had left to prove that even in war they weren't afraid. Edward thought of the times he visited Arras, the city seemed so out of the war. Being so unscathed and untouched made the city look as if no war was going on, and now the war was coming. Edward felt the need to run into the city and demand those that remained to leave, but his place was by his friends preparing to fight the Germans off and keep Arras safe.

The hundred men that traveled by horse back toward new location were scattered with chatter. Each friend talked as if nothing was going on, some talked of their wives back home, others talked about why they signed up to fight. Some sought adventure, others sought to protect their homes and families. Each had their own reasons why they were in this war. Edward tried listening to other conversations while George, Alfred, and Gyles spoke with one another.

Moving the camp from break down to set up took a total of three hours. "Enjoy the night in your cots lads," Captain Hemsworth shouted as the group of a hundred men gathered around him. "Tonight is the last night you sleep in the comfort of your tents, tomorrow we take to the trenches. For those who haven't experienced them yet. keep your heads low and your feet dry."

Edward zoned out once more. He looked over his shoulder at the city their camp set up just outside the city. Captain Hemsworth continued talking but Edward heard none of what he said.

"Well, we should set up then," Alfred said when the company began to disperse through the camp.

"Set up for what?" Edward asked, looking at Alfred slightly confused.

"Weren't you listening?" Alfred asked.

"I know, Hemsworth can be the most engaging speaker," George laughed as Edward looked at his feet. "But to catch you up to speed, we'll be working on the trenches tonight."

"The three of us?"

"Four," Lieutenant Gyles spoke up as they looked at him oddly. "Hemsworth is only making you three to dig the trenches to punish me." The expressions on the men's faces never changed, belying their confusion. "I told him if you're digging, so am I, so it looks like I'm digging," he said.

A light, cold mist began to fall and Edward found himself looking over his shoulder at the city of Arras once more. "Come with me," Lieutenant Gyles ordered Edward, patting his shoulder as he walked toward the city. Edward looked at Alfred then George who nodded toward their Lieutenant, and Edward ran off toward Gyles.

Lieutenant Gyles stopped for a moment and looked behind him. "You too, Alfred," he ordered. Alfred nodded and ran over. The two followed him to their favorite pub.

"Lieutenant Gyles, can you tell us why are we here?" Edward asked as they took a booth closest to the entrance one of the few seats that remained.

"I believe I owe you boys an ending to that story of mine." Edward paused, as excitement ran through his blood. "Now I guess the first thing I should say is that this is the pub I met that pilot," he said as Alfred returned with three beers. "I saw his aircraft fly over us the next day. But I'm getting ahead of myself," he chuckled as Edward took a deep sip from his beer. "I talked to him for a while the night before like I said. I let my men talk to whoever they wanted I was sure they were tired of me. We talked about the new machine that he was flying and how it changed this war. He went on to tell me that the cavalry was a tactic of the past, but I was determined to prove him wrong on that one. The next morning I led my men into war. We were to climb out of the trenches and charge. You know what we did?" Edward and Alfred shook their heads in unison listening carefully. "Well, an hour before we were going to make our run for it...the captain... a face I can see but the name slips me, anyway he ordered that we stand down and continue the attack by shells and mortars."

"So what happened after that?"

"Well we obeyed orders, almost," Lieutenant Gyles sighed, his face clearly had regret all over it. "That lad I was talking to you about a few days ago, he wanted to take a look over the trench. We didn't expect snipers to be looking with all the shells we were dropping on them, so him and I climbed up on the banks of the trench to look over and see the shells falling on the enemy side."

He paused, staring at his beer as if the memory was too fresh a wound. Slowly, he drank from his pint and carefully placed it back on the table, clearly refusing to look at either Edward or Alfred. "We heard the planes," he said. "We both looked behind and that pilot I talked to the day before flew by, we didn't even hear the fire of the sniper. Over the shells falling and the planes it was the perfect distraction. The first bullet missed me, hitting the wall of the trench. I immediately jumped down from the wall and as I reached to pull Oliver down, he already had gotten shot, right in front of me. I watched one of my men die before my eyes. A boy I was in charge of getting through to the end of the war. His knees gave out and fell back limp. The bullet went right through his heart, must have exploded it"

"So... why share this with us?" Alfred asked, his tone slightly surprised and yet intrigued. Edward had thought of Alfred's question too and felt he knew the answer, but still wanted to hear it from Lieutenant Gyles himself.

"Like I said the first day you two were in my company, I am determined to make sure you make it through this war. Your lives have only just begun, it's too soon to see them taken from you. I want to make sure that after this war, there were at least some I got out," Lieutenant Gyles sighed.

"Do you..." Edward stopped as he spotted Adeline enter and walk past their booth. "Ex-excuse me," he said getting up. He made his way to Adeline who smiled as he approached.

"Bonjour," she said.

"Good evening, Adeline," he said solemnly, unsure if the eve of battle was shaking him or simply Gyles' story.

"Pardon, monsieur, but you look, sad," she said slowly, making sure to get her words correct.

"I'm... well," he began, "I fear to ask you something selfish," he said carefully. "But I ask only for your safety. May we talk outside?" She nodded and followed him outside. "I don't know why, but I find myself caring about you a lot these past few weeks," he said as she studied him.

"Pardon?"

"I... like... you," he said slowly, pointing to himself then to her.

"Me?" she pointed to herself, her cheeks getting a light rosy.

He nodded slowly. "That's why I want to ask you to leave Arras," he said carefully as she squinted, he could tell she didn't understand. "Arras," he pointed to the ground. "Leave, go, away from," he said pointing westward. Her head cocked as if she was taken aback.

"Leave? Arras?"

"Oui," he said quickly as she shook her head.

"Je suis infirmière," she said as Edward looked at her funny, not understanding at all what she said.

"The Germans are coming to Arras, Adeline, it's not safe here," he said just as quickly. She clearly didn't understand what he was saying, and both were at a pass of translations.

"Merci," she said holding her hand up. He could tell she was done with their conversation. She turned from him and he reached for her, but she pulled away. "Merci," she repeated her thank you before walking away.

Edward returned to the pub where he found Alfred and Lieutenant Gyles almost finished with their drinks.

"You'd best finish that, before we leave," Alfred said pointing to the nearly filled pint.

"I don't want it, Alf," Edward mumbled as he looked at his friend's empty glass.

"Well if you aren't going to," Lieutenant Gyles laughed, pouring half in his glass and half in Alfred's. "Three weeks here and you fancy someone already," he laughed as Edward ignored the jape.

"Do you remember the pilot?" Edward asked trying to forget about Adeline all together.

"Of course I do, his name slips me, but he did become popular in the beginning of the war."

"So he's still flying."

"I said the beginning of the war. Apparently the Germans shot his plane down. Everyone called him the Seven Arrows. Because he went down with seven arrows. Rumor has it that the arrows are growing though."

"How so?" Edward asked.

"Rumors are going around that after Seven Arrows went down, his son arrived and flew in his father's place with the same insignia on the side of his plane. The boy was young, but learned quickly. They say there's now seventeen arrows in the crow," Lieutenant Gyles chuckled before chugging the remainder of his beer. A small smile appeared on Edward's face. "Apparently, the kid has gumption."

"That's my brother," Edward whispered as Alfred looked at him surprised.

"How are you sure?"

"Alf, I know, my brother told me once that he carried dad's tradition of painting arrows on crows, I didn't know what he meant at the time, but I recall that conversation now," Edward laughed. "I know it's my brother," he smiled. Lieutenant Gyles looked at the clock above the bar.

"And it looks like it's our turn to take the trenches. Are you ready boys?"

"Ready as we'll ever be," Alfred said sternly.

"Let's protect Arras and home," Edward said strongly as the three stood. Edward and Alfred put their caps on and saluted Lieutenant Gyles, who slowly put his cap on.

"I'm honored to serve by your side, gentlemen," he said returning the salute.

Chapter 9

Edward, Alfred, and Lieutenant Gyles left the pub and made their way toward the east side of the city. The temperatures dropped, and the mist turned into snow. Edward rubbed the snow from his eyes. "Looks like we have a long night ahead of us." They all laughed as they made their way through the pasture of their horses as men shouted at each other, herding the groups of horses.

"They're taking them behind the city to keep 'em safe," Edward leaned into Alfred who had a worried look about him. "Blood Stream will be fine, Alf," They met up with George, who handed each of them an entrenching tool. The handle was T-shaped with a spade at the end.

"The ground will be practically frozen," George sighed looking to the sky as the four of them followed the men toward the trenches.

Edward looked across the dark lands of no man's land; silence was the all around as they climbed into the trench with the other men. He dug his spade into the hard soil, slinging a little dirt over his shoulder. It felt as if he made no progress digging at all. The land was in the dead of winter, and digging frozen land was nearly impossible.

"I'd rather be shooting at Jerry," George chuckled as he placed the new duckboards into place.

"You'll be shooting at them soon enough," Lieutenant Gyles sighed as he handed Alfred a sandbag. Alfred handed it to another man, who placed it on the wall to fortify it. Edward walked a few feet ahead to clear out the new path of the trench. He kept quiet, listening to the men he was with. Those that had been in the war for a while and those like him just entering. Each man had his own place and they came from all over. Some told the stories of why they joined. Some were with friends while others just wanted to fight.

"You need help there, Eddy?" a tall skinny man around the age of twenty-one with a New Zealander accent asked.

Edward nodded as he stepped to the side, letting the New Zealander help.

"Frozen land can be a damn pain in the ass, but mud is worse," he said as Edward stuck his spade in the dirt once more.

Edward looked at the man for a moment; he looked older, but the way he talked and acted sometimes gave his age away. In the few hours Edward had been in the trenches, he learned how those around him had acted and carried themselves. He learned their quirks quickly, and he would need to consider he would be working with them till either death took them or the war ended.

"Hell, if this damn war wouldn't have happened," the man stopped stretching backward giving his back a break. He pointed to a scrawny man carrying duckboard. "Ronald there, he would have graduated from University this year, top of his class too. And Arthur," he said pointing to an older looking man digging in a corner of the trench. "He would be working on his farm. Selling his carrots on Saturdays and cabbages on Sundays."

"What about you, Jack?" Edward asked, rubbing his frozen hands together. "What would you be doing if this war never happened?"

"Me?" Jack laughed. Taking his helmet off, he scratched his wet and dirty hair. If it hadn't had been for living in the trenches, his hair would have been blonde instead of dyed brown from mud. "I'd be sitting home, in front of a nice fire. Waiting for a month to pass and then another. So then I could marry Mary Reid, the most gorgeous woman in the world."

Edward chuckled at the statement. "It's true," Jack smiled pulling a picture from his vest pocket. Edward took the photo. A young woman sat proper and poised. She had her ankles crossed and her hands placed on her knees, her blond hair short and purposefully curled and a massive smile on her face. She was indeed a stunning beauty. "Don't smudge it," Jack laughed, taking the photo back and tucking it in his pocket. "So what about you?" he asked. "Got a lass back home?" Edward stopped for a moment. For the first time since leaving England, he thought of Christine. He wondered if she was still mad at him.

"I did," he said carefully as Jack took some duckboard from Ronald.

"Did? You do or you don't," Jack laughed as he began placing the pieces of duckboard in place.

"Well, if you're going to put it that way, I don't. I thought there was, but she was upset with me when I said I was going to enlist. She was a catch, I can tell you that, but not my type of girl."

"Sounds like you fancy another, Eddy."
Edward laughed as he started thinking of Adeline.
Jack laughed louder. "You do. I wish you luck on
your endeavors."

"Shut up and dig," Edward laughed, nudging
Jack who continued to laugh. The men digging
spent the entire night tiring them out and distracting
them from the pain by telling each other stories and
memories of home. By the time dawn came, they
looked at their work. The snow had finally lifted,
and the sun was starting to push its rays through the
clouds on the horizon. A new section of trench had
been nearly completed in one night. Edward leaned
on his entrenching tool, suddenly taken with
exhaustion while soldiers began entering the newly
made trench setting equipment, firearms, and
ammunition up.

"Take a rest for a little, you deserved it,"
Lieutenant Gyles said patting Edward on the
shoulder. "We all do," he added, looking at Alfred
and George who looked just as exhausted as
Edward felt.

As the soldiers filled the trench, those that
worked on it left for the underground areas to sleep.
Edward found himself in the underground tunnels
sleeping in a hard cot, but he didn't care. He slept
through the first bombings while the shaking and
loud sounds of explosions shook the soil above
them. By noon he was shaken awake. "Feeling
rested?" Gyles chuckled as Edward sat up.

"Not really, I feel sick."

"Eat something. Make sure you keep it
down, we're going back."

"We're not digging more are we?" Alfred
asked nervously.

"No we're not. We're planning on crossing no man's land," Lieutenant Gyles said as the group gathered in the sleeping quarters became silent. Every man who had worked through the night who had been awake to hear the words come from Lieutenant Gyles' lips froze in somber silence. Edward thought the call into the day of battle would feel differently. He thought there would be great cheers and chanting. Instead, there was nothing, absolutely nothing.

Edward looked at Alfred who had a face of pure fear. He felt as if the world had stopped. All he could feel was his heart pounding against his ribcage. Slowly he stood as each man slowly gathered his things. Edward quickly took a deep breath, took his VPK out of his chest pocket, and turned to face the men who weren't paying attention to him. Alfred looked up and gave the camera a small smirk just as Edward took the photo.

Tucking his VPK back in his pocket, he grabbed his gun and stood next to Alfred. "Alf, we're going," Edward said sucking in a deep breath.

Alfred remained silent as the group began marching toward the end of the tunnel. With each step Edward's stomach dropped and his heart pounded harder. The sun at the end of the tunnel was blinding. The crack of shrapnel exploding a few yards in no man's land greeted them. The blue sky was hazed with a light fog and smoke from the explosives. Edward stayed close with his group, knowing from training that the trenches were easy to get lost in.

They set up in the section of the trench they had created the night before and sat near the wall as Lieutenant Gyles grabbed the phone on the wall of the trench. Edward noticed Alfred wrap something around his hand, then watched the young man do the sign of the cross. He noticed the rosary, and the sight of his friend praying only made him more unnerved. He took a deep breath as Lieutenant Gyles made his way over to the group.

"These will be our grounds for a little, gentlemen," he said, shouting over another shrapnel shell exploding. "Make sure you keep the ground and heed warnings. Those metal doors," he said pointing to the small metal windows at the top of the trench walls, "must remain closed at all times unless ordered to shoot from one. This is no longer training, this is the real thing." Edward stood up, his palms clammy he jumped a little at the sound of another explosion. "As you were," Lieutenant Gyles sighed glancing at Edward before walking away.

"It's not as bad as I expected," Jack laughed, making his way over to Edward. "A bit noisy, but I'm sure there's not much left of this war. How many more can the German's afford to lose?" he said. Edward felt trapped, worried, and impatient. He couldn't tell if he wanted to run home or shoot a German first. Jack continued talking to him and he simply nodded, not hearing a word his new friend was saying. Jack patted him on the back before walking away. Edward forced a smile before he sat next to Alfred.

"What did he say?" he asked pointing to Jack who was halfway down the trench.

"You weren't listening, well done!"

Alfred laughed. "You seemed into the conversation."

"I have things on my mind," Edward replied, pointing his thumb behind him indicating the Germans less than a hundred meters away.

"I think we all have that on our mind. But you mustn't think too much. You do realize that. Don't think before pulling the trigger. That mustn't… "

"I know that," Edward grumbled. "I didn't think it would be like this."

"Nor did I."

"When I was younger, that is at the beginning of this war. When my father died I had dreams of coming to this place. Fighting and killing the enemy."

"Coming home a hero and the lasses throwing themselves at ya?"

"Exactly." They both chuckled. "But my thoughts on this war started changing a little after Christmas the first year."

"When the newspapers published the photos of the Christmas truce?"

"You saw the enemy as human," George sat next to Edward. "They bleed and die the same. It's definitely a wake up call."

"In the end, it comes down to you or them. Tonight there cannot be a second of hesitation in your actions. Both of you." George leaned forward to look at Alfred. "In the wee hours of the morning, we're attacking. I've heard it from the Lieutenant and Captain. At the sound of the whistles, the gunners will stop and that's when we cross."

"You mean no man's land?" Alfred asked.

"Exactly that," Edward said. "The first day and we're already attempting to cross over."

"We are the last hope Arras has."

"I understand that."

The battlefield went silent. Both machine gun and artillery had stopped completely. Edward looked behind him at the wall of the trench, listening. Silence. The night before, from what he understood, was a simple muse to scare off the Germans. The silence was an awkward feeling. He waited for a bombardment of shrapnel.

"Lads," Lieutenant Gyles cleared his throat as he approached with Jack, the New Zealanders, and a few men that Edward hadn't met yet. "We have our orders," he shouted as Edward faced his Lieutenant. The group that joined Lieutenant Gyles fell into place and sat amongst the 4th Queen's Own Hussars. "Like I said, we have our orders."   No one said a word.

"We are under strict order that tonight our line moves forward. The German front will now become the allied front." Gyles pulled a small crumpled paper from his pocket and unraveled it. "Happy Easter Lads."

Edward blinked dumbfounded. He was surprised he forgot that it was Easter; he never forgot the foundations of his religion. This war had brought thoughts of tradition and holidays to a stop. One day was no different from the next. "Due to it being 8th of April, 1917, Easter Sunday, your orders are to not start until tomorrow. From this moment forth nothing will be done until 05:30 on the morning of the 9th of April." Edward listened intently. "For five minutes the artillery will release there barrages and you will then make an advance on the German lines. God be with you lads. Signed General Henry Horne."

The gathered group sat in silence as Gyles finished reading the letter. The world stood still once more. Edward glanced at Alf, who was digging through his vest pocket, pulling a small Bible out. While he watched his friend, others around them did the same. Some napped while others read. Edward wrote in his journal as the snow began to fall.

Chapter 10

9 April, 1917

I can't think, hell I can barely write right now. What happened this morning, I want to forget it, but I can't. I don't recognize anyone; I think I'm with some of the Canadians. I'm too scared to look for my group. Bloody hell, my hands are shaking so much. The sun just went down and this war has taken the first friend of mine. I hoped it wouldn't be so soon, but at least I know I gave him comfort before he died. I'll start with how it happened.

We've succeeded on our mission. We've not only taken the front line of the German side but the second as well, all in one day. I could barely sleep yesterday and at 05:30 our artillery fired non-stop for five minutes. The sounds of bombs and shells exploding were a wake up call indeed. I told Alf I'd be right next to him the entire time. George nodded at me as he set up the ladder. The trench was small enough but when every soldier stands and files in near the ladders, you really feel the closeness of these trenches.

When the last shell went off, a sharp whistle followed. George was the first one to go over the top. I grabbed the middle rung and looked at Alf giving him a reassuring nod before I climbed over the top.

No man's land was truly hell on earth. The commanding officers worked through the night removing our barbed wire entrapments so that we could cross this morning. Massive craters were sunk deep into the dark black earth. Not a single tree stood in one piece. Empty land stretched for miles. I just thank God the snow that fell was to our backs and in the eyes of our enemies.

We moved slowly and spread out. I sunk into a crater as a gunshot went off, falling onto my hands and knees. In the crater was the body of a French soldier, maybe a few days old. It took everything in my power to keep my mouth shut from giving my location away. When I collected myself and ignored the pungent smell of rotting flesh, I scrambled out of the crater...

10 April, 1917

I couldn't write anymore. I had my first fag to calm my nerves. It felt so soothing, although the taste was awful. I still haven't found my comrades, but the Canadians have shown good hospitality. We've exchanged some fire with the Germans today, but I want to finish what I was writing last night before my nerves got the best of me.

When I climbed out of the crater, I began running toward the German side. A few bodies I didn't recognize were tangled in the barbed wire defenses, some were still alive. I dove into the hard earth as I heard a gunshot go off. I squinted looking at the line of the German defense where I noticed many of our men already jumping into the trench.

Shouts of confusion and what sounded like surrender was coming from the Germans. I spotted a sniper door open, immediately took aim, and shot my rifle at the door. I'm not sure if I hit the man, but the door shut rather quickly. When I noticed the door was closed, I stood up and ran for the trench. My trousers ripped from the barbed wire as I crossed into the pit. That's when I stood with the Canadians.

The Germans looked terrified. Some weren't even fully clothed. I held my rifle to the temple of one who looked maybe four years older than me. I couldn't understand him, but I could tell he was begging for his life. I shouted at him, cursing vulgarity at him. He couldn't understand me as much as I he. At that moment the anger was flowing through me, at that moment I wanted to pull that trigger, but when he continued to beg I realized what I was doing made me no different from them. We took him and many of his comrades under arrest.

The front line was ours in that moment.

Then I saw a few of the Canadians climb up the next wall. They were going for the next line. A commanding officer I do not know by name ordered Myles (one of the Canadians) and I to remain amongst the prisoners. I never felt so relieved. One German who spoke rather good English tried speaking to us, but I was no mood to listen to him and ordered him to keep quiet. Myles, a few of his friends, and I, sat for a while listening to the fighting until it went silent. The first day had been a huge advancement for us, but at what cost? Was this going to help us in the long run? I sure as hell hope so.

By sundown, the war I heard about finally showed its true colors. The part I never wanted to witness. The commanding officers began taking prisoners away when I heard someone asking for help. I could tell I wasn't the only one who heard it because Myles' demeanor changed. He hugged himself and closed his eyes as if he was praying. We knew that whoever was calling for help was dying. We all knew it. The more the person called out, the more I got impatient. As a commanding officer passed by I waited. I knew. If this soldier was going to die, then let it be with one of his own.

When the commanding officer turned around the corner of the trench, I made my way to wall in front of me. Surely this man was shot trying to advance to the second line. Myles and his friends tried to stop me, but after a little convincing I was being pushed up over the top. I stayed as low as possible and began crawling toward the sounds of help. I rolled down into a crater and that's where I found him. George lay in a crater with a broken leg and two bullet holes. He didn't look good, I was surprised he lived this long. God, I still remember our conversation.

"What are the chances of you coming to my aid?"

"We need to get you to a medic."

"A medic won't help. I know what my odds are."

He was never optimistic. I knew that the second I met him a few weeks back. In that moment I longed for the days before the war.

"How's Alf?"

"He's fine, I saw him make it to the second line. He was with the Lieutenant." George had lost so much blood, the snow that still fell blended in perfectly with his skin. "I'm gonna die." He was crying. In the time I knew him, I never knew him to cry. He wasn't the type. I thought him to be an older brother, one who was always collected and never showed weakness. This moment that façade came down. He showed all his weaknesses. "Take it." I hadn't realized he had untied his trumpet from his belt. Deep down I wanted to humor him, make him laugh, but I couldn't think of anything. All I could do was obey his wish. I moved closer and sat next to him. His breathing was shallow. I knew he didn't have much time. "It's been so long I've been at war. About this time the primrose, Lily-of-the-valley, and bastard balm would be blooming."

"And the hills would be covered with them." If I couldn't help him physically, I vowed to help him mentally. "You remember much of home?" He smiled a little. I noticed his lips were stained red from the blood.

"I remember it all. It was my reward at the end of this war."

That broke me, I held it together for him and I let him tell me of his home. George Williams was the oldest of four sons. He lived in Sandwich in Kent. When the war broke out, he and his friends were the first to sign up. He said he hadn't fancied any girl, so he had no heartbreak goodbyes but I somehow doubted him the way he told me every time we talked about the lasses. One time I caught him looking at a photo of him with a young girl so I doubt some of his stories, but that's what made him stand out. George fought because he had people to return to. He fought because he put away his wants and held everyone else's on his shoulders. I remember his selflessness the first time I met him.

After a few minutes of him describing the fields of bastard balm, he stopped talking. I guess it hurt too much. This was one part of war I was not ready for, especially to someone I got to know the past few weeks. A few moments after he stopped talking his breathing stopped and his head fell back. He was gone, and all I remained with was his body. I closed his eyes and sat there with his trumpet for a while. It was a little past sundown when I knew I should have returned.

I said my farewell to my dead friend and comrade and prepared myself to make my way to my trench. I tied the trumpet to my belt as George had done, looked at him one more time, and pulled myself out of the crater. Crawling slowly, I stopped from time to time. The trench wasn't even fifteen meters away, but it looked further.

When I reached the trench, Myles and his friends dragged me in rather forcefully. There was no celebration of my return only awkward silence, and that's when I noticed a commanding officer making his way over. I was ordered night watch with no dinner. He threatened to have me court-martialed but not knowing where my official commanding officer was located, it was simply an empty promise.

After I received my scolding I returned to my seat, this time holding George's trumpet. Myles tried comforting me, but I wanted to keep to myself. He respected my silence and left me alone as well the other Canadians. The rest of the night was long and terrible. From time to time there were bursts of gunfire exchange. From the sounds that came from the new front line we all assumed the Germans were trying to take back their territory.

11 April, 1917

I'm to return to the front lines shortly. This morning
I ran into Jack, whom I worked with building the
trench. He told me Lieutenant Gyles was worried
about his men, since only a handful of them had
made it to the new front line. I was to rejoin my
company, which brought some relief to the
torturous sleepless night. Jack said I should sleep
when I get back to my company, which I agreed.

    I'm shattered; it hurts to look at the ink. But
I wanted to write about my relief before I forgot this
feeling. The relief these fags provide is a new
feeling. I hate the taste, they're terrible, but for
some reason, the shaking in my hands has ceased.
Myles told me it would do that. I look forward to
seeing Alf, but without George we won't be the
same.

                 - Trooper Edward Jacob Poole

Chapter 11

Four weeks into the Battle of Arras, casualties were rising and the tug-of-war battle was endless. The British armies made great advances and then ended up getting pushed back, but their attacks were far more successful than Germany's defenses.

By the start of the fifth week, exhaustion had taken over Edward and his friends. And yet victory felt as if it was on the brink. He found himself leaning against the wall of the trench his eyes half shut. The smells of death, decay, and human excrement no longer bothered them. A smell so terrible was what they knew for the past four weeks. Edward looked at Alfred who slept leaning on the opposite wall. He looked down at the trumpet that hung from his hip. Although George had passed on a few weeks ago, they all felt like he'd come around corner with that smartass smirk. Edward knew he'd never return, but he often hoped.

"You should get some rest," Lieutenant Gyles sighed, making his way over. Edward looked around the trench noticing most of his comrades were sleeping. He shook his head and pulled a fag out. "I need you to be somewhat rested before we make another advancement."

"There is no rest down here." Edward felt as if he was a shell of his former self. The hope and joys of beyond tomorrow were gone. The last advancements he lost three more friends, including Jack Reid from New Zealand. He hardly spoke to anyone and hadn't taken a single picture in days. "What is keeping us alive? Why us?"

"Because by God, you and those who are still working is what keeps your families safe."

Edward opened his mouth to protest, but closed his mouth knowing his Lieutenant was right. Another bombardment of shells exploded above them causing Alfred to burst awake.

"What's going on?" Alfred panted, clenching his rifle.

"German shell fire, Alf," Edward answered. The four weeks they had been fighting everyone's demeanors had changed. The laughing and jokes seemed to die away the more people they lost. Although they died and although their jokes had stopped, one thing kept them fighting. Hope was strong in their spirits. When the bombardment had seized the allied side returned fire. The next few hours would be a stalemate of artillery fire.

A few days past Southeast of their location the town of Monchy-le-Preux had been taken. It was now clear who had the upper hand of this battle. Germany would either risk their entire infantry, or retreat further west defeated. After the artillery fire stopped, Lieutenant Gyles left his men as he did at the same time every day to gather information on movements and placements. Edward looked around. Not even half the faces he saw were familiar.

"William, are you making some char?" he asked a private hunched over a little fire.

The man nodded. "Would you like some?" Edward forced a smile and nodded. For the first time in weeks he reached into his vest pocket and pulled his VPK out. He aimed the camera lens at the man with the teapot and a few exhausted soldiers. Adjusting the window, he captured the image a shell exploding in the background. He jumped a little before putting his camera back in his pocket. When the man finished, he handed Edward a warm cup. "Enjoy."

"Cheers."

"Anything for you, sir."

Edward looked at the man funny.

"You don't remember?"

Edward shook his head.

"You saved my life, sir."

Edward barely remembered what happened the past few weeks trying to suppress the losses of people he knew.

"And how did I do that, William?" he took a sip from his tea leaning on the wall of the trench.

William was a few years older than Edward, but he was constantly sheepish. He kept to himself and often kept silent only to listen. He was only a week new to the war and looked up to everyone, even those younger than him. He knew those longer in the war needed the most respect. "When we crossed over no man's land the beginning of this week. I tripped in a crater and you refused to leave me behind."

Edward nodded, remembering the young man cowering in the crater, a place where no man deserved to be. He told William he had a choice, to keep moving into the machine guns and reach the next line or die in a hole in the ground never seen by another familiar face. Seeing William lying in the crater scared out of his mind only brought the feeling of George dying back. Edward didn't save his life out of kindness rather out of pity.

"He wouldn't stop talking about it for days," someone laughed as a few men joined in.

"Ah bugger off!" Alfred snapped at the one who jested. "You make such vile jokes? Do you not see where we are?"

"Alf."

"No, Eddie!" Alfred snapped holding his hand up. "We aren't just losing soldiers we are losing friends."

Edward sighed. George's loss was effecting his platoon, especially those closest to him like Alfred and Edward.

"We understand our friends, our brothers, and comrades are dying. Each of us lives one day and falls the next," Edward said, looking at Alfred and then to the others. "We understand the loss but we aren't to linger on the loss. What lies beyond that land? That is our goal. We aren't here to tear each other down and joke about cowering and waiting to lose everything. We fight for freedom, for crown and country. I fight for you. I fight for all of you. Will you do the same for me? Will you fight next to me? Or will you all stand back and let me fall? What you make on that battlefield, the decisions large or small, has one of two outcomes. Failure. Success. I do hope you are hoping for success and working toward not only for your sake, but mine as well." The trench became silent. Everyone stared at him in awe. "So now, the next few days we will remember those that have fallen by finishing what they could not. Stay strong my friends, stay strong."

When Edward finished his little speech he
sat back down. Pulling his journal from his pocket,
he began flipping through the little book till he
reached a blank page. Those in the pit with him
returned to their activities, but in silence. No one
said a word out of respect.

When Lieutenant Gyles returned, he ordered
Edward to follow him. Edward closed his journal
and followed after his Lieutenant, looking at Alfred
who shrugged his shoulders. The two men walked
through the trench in silence for a little before Gyles
stopped at the senior officers cooking station. The
smell of bacon and eggs made him feel sick from
hunger. Edward sat on a soapbox and looked at
Gyles who looked at the other men cooking their
breakfasts. "We're making a final push when
exactly?"

"The day after tomorrow, or the day after we
don't know?"

Edward sat quietly as he listened to the
officers speaking with one another.

"And how do we go about this push?"

"The same way we have been. Wait for the
wee hours of the night."

"The last push will be on the 16th of May if
all goes to plan. We will have pushed the Germans
so far back they'll have no choice but to surrender."

"And how can we be so sure?"

"With the success of Monchy-le-Preux a few
days ago, Arras will be ours."

The soft hums of approaching airplanes
silenced everyone. They all looked to the sky.
Through the smoke and cloud they saw allied
fighter jets fly by. Each man let out a small sigh of
relief. Edward watched carefully, squinting to study
each passing plane. They flew low, so each emblem

could be seen if one looked carefully. One plane flew by with eighteen arrows in a black crow. Edward nudged Gyles and pointed up at his brother's plane. A ping of joy shot through him as he watched it fly over the battlefield and off into the distance. He longed for the day to return home with his friends and brother by his side. But he feared that wouldn't be for another six months or more. He felt this war was never going to end.

Captain Hemsworth stepped out from underneath the bunker behind the gathered commanding officers. He whistled, gaining everyone's attention. Pointing at Edward, he wiggled his finger for him to approach. Edward's mind began racing as he waited to be scolded for leaving the trench to go back for George. He stood up and followed Captain Hemsworth into the bunker. "Captain... I..." Captain Hemsworth held his hand, silencing Edward immediately. Then he hunched over a small wooden table with a map of the area. He looked over the map and Edward stepped forward to see what he was looking at.

"We've taken so many of their front lines. Monchy-le-Preux is officially ours. This is our final push," Captain Hemsworth said pointing to the continuous falling German lines. "Some of your comrades have informed me that you have been a whim of encouragement to them."

"I have, Captain?"

Edward found that hard to believe. He simply told them his thoughts and shut down their thoughts of defeat and negativity. He wasn't leading anyone anywhere.

"It was also brought to my attention that you left the trench and crawled away from the battle."

"Captain, I..."

"From what I understand you brought comfort to one of our dying. Is this true?"

Edward looked at the trumpet that hung from his hip and nodded silently.

"Don't do it again. But you did a good thing." Captain Hemsworth returned his sight to the map and pointed to where Edward's section was. "By general law what you did was technically desertion, but I am willing to let the notion die." Edward bowed his head saying nothing. "Now, consider this a test for you. When you return to your lines, pick four men you trust and give them the exact orders I am giving you."

For the next twenty minutes, Captain Hemsworth spoke with Edward of what they would be doing on the morning of the 16th. "At 04:25 the allied side will make advancements on the German's side after a set of artillery fire. This final push will take the German side and push them further back to the point of victory for our side."

Edward understood exactly what the Captain was asking of him. He was quickly informed that this was a test of his suitability for a promotion to Lance Corporal. Edward didn't understand why they were choosing him. He simply did what was asked of him and nothing more. He wasn't special. When Captain Hemsworth had finished speaking, he was released. Lieutenant Gyles stood by the fire with the other officers.

"Need a smoke?" he asked as Edward pulled a fag out. "I have the light." Lieutenant Gyles took his matches out and lit Edward's fag. "I suppose congratulations is in order."

"For what?" Edward asked blankly letting a soothing cloud of smoke out. Lieutenant Gyles looked at him. "Why me? Is it through a shortness of men that they choose me?"

"Absolutely not." Edward took a glance at Lieutenant Gyles. "It was partly on my request. You've proven in this single battle your capabilities, your compassion. You risked your life to try to save George. Honestly, the others look up to your courage."

Edward had seen none of his friends looking up to him the way his Lieutenant boasted. He simply saw them as friends, but he appreciated what the Lieutenant was saying. He thanked him and made his way back unaccompanied. He kept quiet on his return, although he could see his friends wanting to know where he went.

He lowered the brim of his helmet trying to get some rest and woke at half one in the morning. Most of his friends slept on, while some sat reading from pocket Bibles. He walked to one of the sleeping men and kicked his foot, instantly waking him. He held his finger to his lips and helped the man up.

"William, get Alf and meet me here." William nodded, exhaustion in his eyes. Edward woke another and told him to stand with Alfred and William. He then made his way to another who sat reading from his Bible.

"Go away, Poole," the man sighed, turning the page.

"I want you to know what's going on, James."

"I know what's going. We're shooting Jerry while pushing their arses back. That's all I need to know."

"What if I had information that said we could move on from this place?"

"That would be some good information, but somehow I doubt it."

"James, I'm going to need your help." James Wilson looked up, the expression of suspicion clear in his grey-green eyes. He was taller than Edward and seven years his senior. His matted brown hair curled and crusted from the mud and was often slicked back or tucked under a helmet.

James closed his Bible and placed it in his pocket. "I'm guessing where you've gathered privates Alf, William, and Liam?"

Edward smiled a little and nodded. The two walked to where the other three gathered.

Liam was a scrawny young man around the age of twenty. His beard was no more than peach fuzz. He took his helmet off and ran a hand through his copper hair. "What exactly are we doing?" he yawned.

"I'll tell you." Edward leaned against the wall looking at his friends and comrades. "I've chosen the four of you for a simple reason, to give you insight what will happen soon. All that I ask is your help." The four men looked back at him like stone.

"Well get on with it," James said impatiently. From the lack of sleep James was getting, it was clear what was driving his nerves to their limits.

"We, along with the rest of the front line, will be attacking the last of German sides in a few days. My orders are to lead the four of you into this final battle. After artillery fire that morning, we are to cross the final stretch of no man's land, no earlier or later. As long as I still stand I promise you all the same."

"You can't make a cheap promise," James sighed.

"I can make a promise I know I'm going to keep. I simply chose you four since we've grown close these past few weeks." The next twenty minutes Edward spoke with his men sternly but carefully. He wanted their respect, and in their eyes he saw that he already had it. They listened to what he wanted and the power of giving orders only felt natural. He wondered if he was only being promoted because so many had died and they needed more leaders, but that thought quickly passed and he continued speaking with his men as he always had. They spoke simply, as old friends. Well, most of them did. James simply listened. They shared stories of home and got to know each other better. In a few days the final test would prove how strong the British army was and how well Edward could lead a squad.

Chapter 12

As the hour drew near, Edward looked up from his journal. James and William slept in front of a small fire while Alfred and Liam were talking. Edward checked his pocket watch and saw the attack would start shortly. He closed his journal, tucked it in his pocket and pulled his VPK out.

"Alf," he whispered, pointing to his sleeping comrades. Alfred smiled and nodded. Edward watched as his friend crawled and sat next to William. "Liam, you too." Liam looked at Alfred and Edward with a confused look. When he noticed Edward holding his camera, he nodded and began crawling to the opposite side of James. Edward opened the window of his VPK to get as much light from the fire to develop the photo. Alfred and Liam smiled as Edward took the photo.

"I swear, you put anything on me or in my mouth, I'll kill you. German or ally," William grumbled.

"Ditto," James added. The two men opened their eyes looking around blankly. "What time is it?"

"Quarter past four. Almost time. Thought you could use the rest," Edward answered, tucking his VPK into his pocket. Further down the trench someone cooked eggs and when the smell reached them Edward gagged. The smell of cooked food, death, and other bodily functions was not a pleasing smell. The taste of food alone could make one sick at that moment.

"Can we go over this one more time?" William asked, fear plane as day in his eyes. Edward nodded benevolently.

"The storm will begin with artillery fire in just under fifteen minutes. Our final push will get us in the town of Feuchy. What I want from the four of you is to stay spread out. Do not bunch together. Easier targets that way. Once we've breached their line and push them into the town, we'll push them out like ants. They'll have no place to go. Prisoners, death, or retreating, those are their three options. Hell, I don't know why they don't just give up now." Edward felt a swarm of confidence as he spoke to the four men who listened intently. "William and James, I want both of you behind me and Liam and Alfred I want you two behind them. Understood?"

"Yes, sir," they all said all at once. He smiled at the sound of their voices. He was a born leader and the few months he had been at war he could already feel a surge of change. He was no longer the innocent boy longing for a fight. He was stronger and harder, and commonly cursed more. His family was sure to not recognize him on his return, and his teachers would be surprised with his vernacular too. He turned his back to his men and placed his hand on a sandbag supporting his entire body weight. He closed his eyes momentarily, mumbling a prayer or two.

He dozed off a little, and the rumbling and pounding of explosives caused him to jolt awake. He looked at his stopwatch, seeing it was only twenty-three minutes past the hour. Edward turned and faced his men. All four had a look of worry. He forced a smile before he left to retrieve a ladder. As he returned, he witnessed a solider vomit from stress. He shook his head and returned to his men. "While we stand we fight, we don't go down till our last breath leaves us."

"Aye," James yelled as the others nodded. Edward placed the ladder against the wall of the trench. The ground vibrated from the pounding of the shells exploding over the Germans. "Those Jerry have another thing coming." Edward looked at his pocket watch again; the firing had been going on for three minutes. He placed his foot on the bottom rung and looked at his men.

"Stay in formation, take your time, and I'll see you in Feuchy."

The men nodded.

Two minutes later, the gunfire stopped. However, the silence was only brief before a high pitch whistle blasted. Edward took a deep breath as he began climbing the rungs of the ladder. No man's land was not the same image of earlier crossings. Here the land looked more like land. Patches of grass and flowers scattered across the surface. Trees stood full, while a few had split and burned. Scars of war trudged the earth here but not as noticeable as the land to their backs.

Edward marched onward, with William and James behind him as instructed and Liam and Alfred behind them. Every time Edward exhaled as he crossed, a cloud of vapor spurred out. He thought of a fag as he got halfway. The return of Jerry fire began. Machine gun and rifle bullets flew by. The sound was close, but the bullets practically invisible. The sound of a soft whistle blew past his ear. His heart stopped momentarily at the sound, knowing the bullet came too close. Behind him, he heard a sick thump followed by a horrific scream. He glanced over his shoulder as he watched James grab his leg and collapse. "Shit." He looked at the other three, ordering them to keep moving. They were almost there. "Keep going!" he yelled.

"What are you doing?" James grumbled, holding his leg.

"I'm not leaving any of my men behind."

"You are stupid, you know that, kid?"

"Shut up. Can you stand on it?" He looked at the bullet hole in James' thigh. He looked over his shoulder again seeing Alfred, Liam, and William jumping into the enemy pit with a few more unknown men. He smiled a little; the mission was already going according to plan. Arras was almost in their total control. The machine guns had stopped. The allied side was too much inside the trench for the enemy to worry about no man's land. "Come on," Edward demanded, struggling to lift James.

The older man leaned on him helping to lift with his good foot and the two began moving as fast as they could. Taking five minutes, they reached the trench where a full out fight was already underway. Edward lowered James into the trench. James pulled his handgun out. Edward did the same as he leapt down. In his hand he held a Webley MK VI revolver ready for use and fully loaded.

Few Germans had begun the retreat. Edward looked around a confusion of gunfire and piles of bodies from both sides. He suddenly noticed Alfred pinned to the wall fighting a German with a knife. Without hesitation, he aimed his gun and fired. The German collapsed leaving Alfred frozen to the spot, staring at the dead body. "You're welcome, Alf," Edward smirked.

But the smirk quickly faded when another German ran toward Edward. Again without thinking he fired, watching as the body fall before him. Shouts of surrender came from a few Germans who placed their weapons down as others began retreating for Feuchy. The trench was theirs. It happened so quickly but the weakened side fighting five weeks could go on no more. Edward knew it was time to take back Feuchy. He looked at James who sat by himself in the emptied trench. "Stay with the prisoners until my return or a commanding officer comes to retrieve them."

"I don't think I have much of a choice."

Edward smiled and returned his attention to the others. "This is it lads, our final push. Feuchy just lies beyond this trench. Take it and Arras is safe in our hands. Remember keep your distances apart and move quickly, stay low when you need to."

William, Liam, and Alfred all nodded and began climbing the back banks of the trench pulling over the top. "We'll be back."

James waved him onward telling him to leave. The whole thought of the first battle being over so quickly brought some joy to Edward. He spotted his three men running ahead and began sprinting in their direction. As he entered the small town he spotted the remains of an old church, the crucifix was the only thing left standing. An explosion echoed out in the distance as he saw all three of his men enter a building. Another explosion brought his attention to a burning ruin. He thought of what the house looked like and how long it would be before the house could be livable again after the war. A rifle shot echoed out, bringing him back to the present and forcing him to put the thoughts of the future in the past.

He ran to where he last saw his men, entering through the front door rifle aimed and ready for any surprise. The small home was filled with a light cloud of smoke from a small fire in the roof. Liam shouted, pointing his bayonet at Edward who quickly knocked the blade away from him.

"S-sorry sir," Liam said embarrassed, as Edward held his hand up.

"No need for apologies now. You just keep yourself alive."

Liam nodded nervously, the look of embarrassment still on his face. William and Alfred stood by the window looking out intently.

"It's too quiet."

"They're in retreat," William sighed. Edward walked toward them.

"See anything?"

"No," both Alfred and William said.

"Keep looking."

A soft shuffle scraped the ceiling. Edward looked up as the shuffling stopped. "Liam," he whispered, pressing one finger to his lips while pointing to the ceiling. "Come with me. Alf, William, stay down here and be vigilant." Edward rested his rifle on the wall and pulled his handgun out.

He and Liam started up the stairs, stopping halfway to listen. Someone scrambled in an unseen room. "Stay back a little." Edward didn't want to risk Liam's life. He made it to the landing of the top of the stairs and slowly made his way down the hall.

He entered a room at the end where he found a teenaged boy cornered. He wore a German uniform; his hand shook as he aimed his gun at Edward.

"Put it down," Edward demanded, aiming his gun at the boy. The boy was white as a ghost and sitting in the corner of the room.

"Um gnade bitten," the boy said nervously. Edward couldn't understand him.

"Put the gun down," He said again as the German continued to repeat his plea. It didn't take Edward long to realize the boy was begging for mercy.

"Ich will nicht sterben." Fear was plain in the boy's eyes.

"Put the gun down!"

The boy jumped and threw the gun away.

"Um gnade bitten, bitte, bitte!" He was shaking violently now.

"Liam, get the gun," Edward ordered as his friend moved slowly toward the frightened German, both men watching carefully to see if the boy would do something irrational. Liam retrieved the boy's gun and scrambled behind Edward. "Go back down stairs, when you see the military police pass the house, bring them here."

Liam nodded and ran down the stairs as Edward stared intently at the boy. He was only a couple of years younger than him. Edward wondered where he came from, where he lived before the war, and why he joined so young. He then thought about how when he was a couple of years younger and the war just started, he wanted to go fight for king and country.

"You smoke?" he asked as the German looked at him oddly. He reached in his front pocket holding a fag in the air. "You smoke?" Edward repeated putting the unlit fag to his lips.

The German nodded and Edward tossed him one. He lit his and threw the matches at the German. Edward took a deep inhale and let the warm smoke sink into his lungs before blowing it out. He looked out the window. "Where are you from?" he asked knowing that he would not get an answer. The German sat frightened in the corner smoking while staring at Edward. "Where in Germany do you live?" Still he received no communication from the German. He sighed and sucked in some more smoke. He returned his attention to the window as he watched a fellow soldier run through the street to another house. Edward wondered how long he would be sitting in this house. Across the way, he spotted a German sneaking around another building. Not too long after spotting the German he heard rifle fire echoing through the house. The man tried retreating, but was too late and was shot down. The firing in the house seized and Edward returned his attention to the boy.

"You have a name?" he asked as the boy sat smoking. "Mine's Edward," he said patting his chest.

"Wilhelm," he said back copying Edward. Finally, a verbal answer. The next hour went on for what felt like an eternity. By dawn, the small town of Feuchy was absolutely still. No soul, allied or enemy, moved. Edward wondered if any Germans remained alive besides Wilhelm.

"Sir," Liam called from the base of the stairs. Edward looked at Wilhelm, who didn't look as frightened anymore. Liam walked into the room. Silence took over; Edward glanced out the window once more. The soldiers of Great Britain started filling the streets cheers of celebration filling the air. "They've retreated, Feuchy is ours as well as Arras. We won."

Edward nodded. Sighing, he stood up. Although deep in his heart he wanted to do nothing more than to release Wilhelm, he knew that to be a traitorous act. He stood the German up and pushed him in the direction of the door. The three men made their way to the lower level of the house. William and Alfred gave the German a dirty look before they all left the house. They walked the streets until they found a few military policemen.

"We found this one cowering on the second floor with no weapon to defend himself," Edward said, presenting Wilhelm to one of the men.

"But..."

Edward grabbed Liam's wrist, shutting him up.

"Right, thank you men," the leader of the MP saluted them and the four returned the salute. "As you were." Edward nodded and led his group to where they left James.

"Why did you claim him unarmed?" Liam asked slightly frustrated.

"Because he was."

"Yes, after we unarmed him."

"Sometimes, Liam, you do things to lessen a punishment on someone. Take for example your horse. You wouldn't shoot it dead because it had a small scratch on its hind, would you?"

"No... sir, I wouldn't but I don't understand why you claimed him unarmed."

"He is a prisoner of war. He will be treated just the same as any prisoner, except a little better by declaring he hadn't pointed a weapon at us." Liam became silent after Edward's arguments.

Alfred stepped forward, walking side by side with Edward.

"We made it through."

"The battle, yes. But Alf, the war is far from over." Edward felt frightened but refused to show or speak of it. "We've lost some friends already. George, Jack, and some other great men."

"And now they have their eternal reward. But tonight we celebrate a little. Head into town... what's left of it."

"Maybe." Edward was in no mood to celebrate. Sure they experienced their first victory, but they were far from safe. Soon, they'd be picking up their equipment and horses and moving to the next location, wherever that may be.

Eventually, through snow and cold, they made it back to the last trench they took. The trench was nearly empty except for those scavenging through German equipment or wounded. They found James sitting with a few medics examining his leg.

"What news?"

"Arras and Feuchy are ours. Germans retreated. We've won." For the first time since Edward met him, James smiled. Seeing this brought a little relaxation to Edward. The five men sat down with him and Edward listened as Liam, William, and Alfred shared their experiences of the morning.

"Poole!" Captain Hemsworth shouted from the Southern end of the Trench.   Edward rose slowly and made his way toward the man. The more he relaxed, the more tired he became. His walking slowed, and he began yawning. Now that he was no longer on guard and the adrenalin did not flow, he was giving in to the exhaustion. He wanted nothing more than to lie right then and there and sleep.

When Edward reached Captain Hemsworth, the captain said nothing only turned around and began walking away. Edward, tired and numb, yawned again and followed after him. The two men approached a group of several Lieutenants and Majors. Lieutenant Gyles was amongst them. Lieutenant Gyles immediately shook Edward's hand. For several minutes, Edward stood frozen amongst the other men. Now that he was Lance Corporal, he could hear more information than a Trooper could. When the men had ceased their conversation and shook Edward's hand, they left and returned to their sections.

"Congratulations," Lieutenant Gyles said shaking Edward's hand again. "You're lucky, not all Lance Corporal's keep all their men. You're lucky one got out with just a leg wound."

"Will he be able to return home?"

Lieutenant Gyles shrugged.

"I doubt it, they've examined James' leg. After it heals they'll probably return him to the front lines. You'll need to choose another person to replace him."

Edward nodded solemnly. He had no thought of replacing James just yet.

Edward and Lieutenant Gyles walked down the trench; the stress of battle was no longer on anyone's shoulders. "We'll remain here a few days, make sure the Germans do not try another force," the lieutenant said. Edward nodded silently. He looked around at some passing medics carrying a body out of the trench. His mind began thinking of the loss.

"Do we have a number on casualties?" He thought of George at the escape of his own question. He hated the thought of him dying, although he wasn't alone. Edward grabbed his friend's trumpet that hung from his belt.

"We've lost a lot of men. Roughly a hundred thousand and climbing."

Edward felt a small sharp pang in his chest.

"A lot of great men."

"Don't let it hinder you. Remember them, but don't let it destroy you. You'll never forgive yourself for something you didn't even do." Edward knew Lieutenant Gyles' words were true, but he still couldn't get over the death of his friends. As they returned to Edward's remaining men, everyone stood stiff at attention. "I present you lads, your Lance Corporal Edward Poole." Alfred smiled instantly. The three men saluted before patting him on the shoulder.

"We couldn't have done what we did without you," William said as Gyles laughed. Edward wouldn't allow the ego of a promotion to go to his head, so he sat down by the fire boiling a pot of water.

"Well, I'm glad you lads think so highly of me." William, Liam, and Alfred sat next to the fire. "But... let's not talk of promotions or war. Tell me about yourselves. Your homes and families." Edward caught a smile on Lieutenant Gyles' face as the older man sat on an upturned box and joined them. For the next hour they all shared stories of home. Liam was living just outside Southampton on a farm when the war broke out. His father was dying, so he refused to enlist to take care of his father. When his father died a year into the war, he took care of his sisters and mother as well the farm. When all his friends left for war and he was being heckled day in and day out by the enlisters, he finally caved and signed up.

William lived in London and was studying Architecture at the University of London. He signed up six months into the war. He wasn't afraid, but because he was attending university, he could have remained in the country to finish his degree without going to war. William knew his degree would be waiting for him on his return.

It astounded Edward how different each man was, and yet war brought everyone together. They talked of patriotism and home as if they were there. They made jokes and took to laughing like old friends. Now that the stress of battle was over for the day, they could let their guards down temporarily.

Chapter 13

As night fell, Edward stood and stretched. He looked at his men. "Anyone care to join me at the pub?" Without a hesitation, all three stood up causing laughter amongst them. "I'll take that as a yes."

The four of them climbed out of the trench and made their way to town. When they entered the city of Arras, the blown out buildings and damaged roads made the city look completely different. People roamed the streets like haunted beings unsure where to go. They made their way to the pub. The front of the building no longer existed, but still soldiers gathered there drinking, cheering, and laughing.

"First round's on me," William said as Edward held his hand up. "Sir, I insist." Edward chuckled as the four men walked into the crowded building. Liam found room in the back of the building and took the table with Alfred, while William and Edward waited at the bar to be served.

Edward looked around trying to see if he could spot Adeline, but she wasn't there. "Amazing how the building got destroyed and yet, we're all gathered here to celebrate." Edward silently nodded, finally giving up on his search. He wondered if she'd arrive later than she often did. When they finally were served, the men took the four pints back to their table.

"To our success," Alfred said holding his pint up.

"And more to come!" William added.

"To James," Edward added.

"And the lucky bastard who'll replace him," Liam finished as the men laughed and clanked their glasses together. Edward took a massive gulp and slammed his mug down.

"God," he sighed leaning back. "Never thought this war was going to be so stressful."

Liam laughed. "I thought the exact same when I enlisted," he said. "The work was tiring and the training in the rain was God awful. I thought Mist was going to drop dead the first day."

"Well at least your horse knew how to jump a stream."

"He flew right over Frosty Queen's head and fell in the stream," Alfred laughed.

"Yes, and thanks for reminding me, mate," Edward shook his head taking another gulp of his beer. "I think she can do it now, but getting her to that stage was difficult. I mean we had a full two weeks of training before being thrown into the trenches."

"My question," William cleared his throat. The men gave him their attention as he drank. "Do ya have an idea who you're going to get to replace James?"

Although they were all together, they weren't a full unit without James and everyone knew it. Of course, Edward hadn't given much thought on whom to replace him. He shook his head taking another drink. The others shrugged. They all continued to share stories of how they enlisted and whom they enlisted with. Both William and Liam enlisted with their pals but for some reason joined the cavalry while their friends joined other branches. Alfred and Edward were the only ones they knew thus far that enlisted alone.

"May I join you lads?" They all looked up from their table and noticed a copper headed boy no older than fifteen standing before their table. He clearly wasn't enlisting age, but everyone knew the enlisters took whatever they could get. His uniform was clean. By the look of his uniform, he was clearly new to the 4th Queen's Own Hussars. "Lieutenant Hannah Gyles instructed me to find the pub and meet some of the lads." Liam chuckled at the use of Lieutenant Gyles full name. Edward kicked his shin under the table.

"Careful with the steal," Liam laughed as Edward stood and offered his seat.

"Cheers," the young man said as Edward leaned against the post behind him. "I'm Charlie Bartle," The boy smiled as each went around the table introducing themselves.

William glanced at Edward, who stared at Charlie listening to him. Charlie went on to tell them that he came from Dover. He clearly wasn't the strongest, but he was willing to fight and that's what they needed most. He was scrawny and his helmet was too big. Alfred took Charlie's helmet off and placed it on the table.

"Did ya come with a horse?"

"Aye, Silver Eye is his name. I was instructed to tie him up with the others." They hadn't spoken much of their horses in the trenches and now Edward felt a longing to see his horse. He finished his beer and leaned back listening to his friends. In the back of his mind he thought of Frosty Queen and wondered how well she was.

"Who wants another round? Lance Corporal?" Alfred nudged Edward who gave him a sideways glance. Charlie immediately stood up and saluted as the four remaining men began laughing.

"Look what ya did, Alf," Edward laughed. "Charlie, stand down." They were all in a riot of laughter. When the men around the table collected themselves, Edward stood up. "I don't know about you lads, but I want to see my horse. I'll have another round after that." Alfred stood up indicating he'd come too. Edward looked at Liam and William who remained at the table. "Hold our seats then?" Liam raised his mug before taking another sip.

"May I come?" Charlie asked hesitantly.

Edward nodded and made his way for the exit. The three of them made their way through the streets of Arras. Some buildings were still smoking from the attacks of the past month. They walked through the blown out streets in silence. Edward tucked his hands in his coat pockets. In the distance, they could hear faint whinnies coming from the horses, and an uplifting feeling filled his entire being. It brought a certain joy to know that something good still lived through tragedy.

When they spotted the horses, they quickened their pace. Edward was the first to reach the team. He found Frosty Queen prancing in place when she spotted him.

"Hey, girl," he whispered petting her behind the ear. She nudged his chest sniffing him for snacks. "I don't have anything," he laughed.

"Here," Charlie said. Edward looked over to the boy who held a sugar cube in his palm. "I brought some for Silver Eye, but yours can have one."

"Cheers," Edward smiled. He took the sugar cube and gave it to Frosty Queen who ate it as if she hadn't seen food in years. He rubbed her nose as he pressed his forehead to hers. He closed his eyes, wanting to remain with her for a while. Then he turned and faced Alfred, who was hugging Blood Stream's massive neck. He smiled as Frosty Queen nudged him, nearly knocking him over. He continued petting her nose. When he looked at Charlie, he said, "Are you apart of a section?"

"A section?" Charlie asked. He was clearly not seasoned to the military yet, and Edward simply smiled.

"Very well," Edward shook his head. "You'll be with me and my section."

"Your section?"

Edward simply nodded.

"You want me? Why?"

"Why not?" Edward smirked, looking at Alfred. "My section is a pretty close nit group. And I tend to keep a close eye always protecting my lads." He kissed Frosty Queen on the nose. "I think we should head back to the pub."

Without saying anything else Edward began walking back into town with Alfred and Charlie right behind him. They returned to the pub, where they found Liam and William still at the table with five full mugs of beer sat in the center.

"We knew you were coming back," Liam said as Alfred and Edward took one. Charlie stood awkwardly while everyone stared at him.

"You're going to want to drink that," Edward said pointing to the last beer.

"I haven't drunken anything before."

"Well, believe me you're going to want to start." Everyone laughed at Edward's comment. When Charlie picked up the beer, Edward raised his. "For the lives lost this past month, and to our very own James Wilson for his recovery."

"For James," Liam, William, and Alfred said.

"For James," Charlie said hushed. Everyone drank deeply from their beers. Alfred took his seat and Edward afforded Charlie his. Edward looked around the pub as they all talked the next few hours. He studied the faces that gathered at the bar and tables. Barely any of them looked familiar. He wondered how many of them had sat at the tables a month before the battle began.

"Isn't that right, Lance Corporal?" Liam asked. Edward shook his head and looked at the four men.

"Pardon?"

"We were just discussing with Charlie here, how we won the battle. He doesn't believe that it took us only five weeks."

"Oh, right, well of course it took us five weeks, a lot of men lost because of our pushes. But many o' Jerry caught." His friends chuckled, raising their glasses. He smiled meekly and placed his empty mug. "If you lads will excuse me?"

"Oh right, going…"

"Stay, enjoy yourselves. Believe you me, you all deserved it. I simply want to go on a walk. I'll see you back in the trench," Edward said calmly. His men looked at him quietly before nodding.

Edward walked past the table and left the building. He strolled through town looking at the half blown-out buildings, studying those that still burned. He wondered about the war and how long it would continue. He thought of the German boy and wondered why neither of them shot. He thought of the next time he did that the outcome may not be the same. Visions of his first battle began coming to mind. The first man he ever shot emerged. He found it astounding how quickly life left the body. His hands began to shake as he numbly walked the streets.

"God," he whispered. "How many more will die?"

He looked to the night sky, listening to the silence. "Forgive me, forgive me for the ones I've killed and will kill."

He stopped walking and looked at his trembling hands. The war had already changed him, so quickly. He knew no longer of being innocent. That was gone now. He was stronger and harder in both physique and mental capacity. He wondered if this was the maturity his brother Andrew spoke of. Thinking of his brother, he pulled a letter from his pocket. The letter was addressed to his brother. He had written several letters back home and often thought to send one to Andrew, but knew he'd never see it, so he kept it with him. He read the letter to himself over and over. "So this is war?" he spoke up, looking around tucking the paper back into his pocket. "Tomorrow we no longer know where we will be and no longer care. As long as we live through tomorrow we can see another day." Taking another fag out, he lit it. Smoking, he made his way back to his trench.

The cold was bearable and none of the five men discussed the weather. Edward listened as they talked of sweethearts back home and how William received another letter, although Edward thought

the lass was made up since William never showed
them the letters. "Ah, you're just telling stories
again, there isn't a lass waiting for ya back home,"
Liam said as they all laughed except for William.

"There is, I tell ya."

"If there is, where are her letters?" Alfred
asked.

"To hell with both of ya," William grumbled
as he quickened his pace to get ahead of them.

"Alright lads, take it easy," Edward started.
"Even though the only relationship he can keep is
with his rifle, and even she wants to get out of his
hands," Edward said as his comrades roared in
laughter. William began laughing too, knowing the
joke was funny.

Chapter 14

As dawn approached, Edward sat in the trench picking cooties from his shirt secretly wishing for a nice, long, hot shower. He looked up from his shirt at his sleeping mates from time to time, wishing he had someone to talk to. "Cootie search?" Lieutenant Gyles asked as Edward looked up scratching his back.

"Can't get rid of the bastards."

"True, but they seem to have grown with me, I hardly realize they're there."

"Except when the big ones bite down." Both men laughed, waking some of those sleeping around them.

Lieutenant Gyles glanced at his pocket watch. Edward noticed and asked what time it was.

"Quarter past six. We are to be leaving soon?"

"We are?"

"We're heading to Cambrai. Except not immediately."

"What is that supposed to mean?"

"There is a forest half a day's ride from here. Just northwest. We are to camp there for the next two or three nights make sure the road to Arras is safe. Then we are to make our way back south to Cambrai. I'd suggest you wake your men soon." Without saying another word Lieutenant Gyles left Edward and moved to another part of the trench.

Edward thought for a while. Deep in his gut, he felt a nervous pulse but this was war and those nervous pulses were frequent. He shook the feeling away, rose and began waking his men. He instructed them on what they were doing and where they were going. Charlie was the most nervous, and the rest of the group noticed.

"Cheer up lad, this is the easy part," William said nudging him.

"He's right," Edward said. "We're simply relocating our horses setting up camp for a few days and then breaking it all down and returning to the battle."

"He's fresh to war," Liam said.

"We know that, he hasn't seen what has happened," Alfred added.

"Can we focus on getting the horses?" Edward snapped as his group stiffened.

"Sorry, sir," Liam mumbled.

Edward waved his hands, indicating for them to move. They all left the reserve trench and began making their walk across town to gather their supplies and horses. Their spirits were high and not much had crossed their minds that morning. Edward thought fondly of where they were to be going. The safety of the forest made him feel secure, enclosed within the woods no one would be able to spot them.

When they reached the horses, they found accompany already there.

"A little late, don't ya think?"

"It's never late when it comes to war, we arrive when we intend to," Edward joked as someone else laughed.

"Just because he got a promotion, he thinks he's high and mighty."

"Bugger off," Edward laughed.

The men teased and picked at each other's problems on a daily basis, a way of keeping their spirits up. No harm came from their jests, but Charlie looked as if they insulted each other. "It's all for the laugh," Edward whispered to the young soldier who nodded quietly still looking confused.

Edward looked around at the cluster of men and horses and quickly pulled his VPK out. Sprinting a few feet away he adjusted the lens and aimed it at the group before taking a quick shot. "Alf, William, Liam, Charlie over here," he called out. The four men approached and lined up for a picture.

"Get in here, will ya," Alfred laughed, waving Charlie over. He sheepishly joined the group for the photo. After Edward took the photo and the three men returned to their horses, Charlie walked with Edward.

"I thought there was ban on those?"

"There was and still is, but as long as the commanding officer doesn't see, we're fine," Edward laughed patting Charlie on the back.

They walked back to their horses. Blood Stream reached out, nudging Edward as he passed. Alfred laughed as Edward caught himself from tripping. "I'll remember that Blood Stream," he said, patting the horse's nose as Blood Stream snorted. "Yeah, you too. Keep him in line, will ya?" he asked the horse as he pushed Alfred. Blood Stream neighed as if he, too, was laughing.

Edward finally made his way to Frosty Queen, kissed her nose, and untied her. He had his things packed the day before while waiting orders and climbed on his horse.

"Alright lads, we have a long day ahead of us," Lieutenant Gyles barked sitting atop his horse. "We'll be making our way to the forest east of Arras. We will then remain there for a few days making sure no German was left behind. Then we will meet the rest of the Army at Cambrai. Understood?"

"Yes, sir!" the company echoed in unison. One by one, they mounted their horses, Edward's group staying close to him. Slowly, they made their way out.

The ride was going to be long, and Edward wanted nothing more than order amongst his group and for the most part that was what he got. The men lined their horses two by two and followed the one in front of them. Not much was said apart from a few jokes from time to time to keep their spirits up, some passed cigarettes, while others sang. Edward daydreamed. He thought of home, and wondered what his family was doing at that moment. He remembered home before the war, the town busy and everyone always happy. He thought of his friends who had died before he enlisted, trying to remember what they looked like. He couldn't see many of them, the years had taken their features away.

He started thinking of Gavin, hoping he was alive. He looked forward to the day of returning to the local pub and drinking with his best friend. For the first time since leaving England, he thought of Christine. A little part of him missed her, but leaving on different terms he knew it was over. She refused to say goodbye, knowing that he may never return. It hurt a little knowing that she was so angry with him that she wouldn't say a last farewell. "Do you have any regrets when you left home?" Edward asked, looking at Alfred.

"What do you mean?"

"It's a pretty straight forward question, Alf. People you never said goodbye to, something you should have done before you left?"

"Oh, well when ya put it like that, no. Not really. Why do you?"

"Only one. I regret not finding a friend to say goodbye to. We didn't leave on good terms."

"And now we're here not knowing if we'll ever return home." To Edward the words that Alfred spoke sounded worse than his inner thoughts. He humbly nodded without answering. "Well, why not write this friend, I mean you send letters home all the time, but it's only to your family. Try sending one to this friend." Edward smirked. "I mean, I send at least one letter to my friends back home and it makes me feel better. Yeah, I wish I was back home with them, but someone needs to be here."

"We are the front," Edward whispered looking ahead and trying to see the leading horses.

"Exactly."

Edward smiled knowing his friend hadn't understood what he meant. They themselves were becoming the front line protecting the trenches from potential invaders. The Germans had pulled back significantly after their lose at Arras, and now it was up to Edward and his company to hold the front until the reserves reached them. He realized they were sent to the forest first because they were on horseback and could get there faster than any other mobile force.

Above them, four low-flying allied planes flew by. Edward recognized the three behind the leader but the leader was a new plane. An unsettling feeling sunk down in the pit of his stomach. They all watched as the planes flew further east.

"You all right?"

"I'm fine, Alf," Edward cleared his throat staring as the planes faded to dots and soon vanished. He returned to his inner thoughts, dreaming of home. The more he thought about home, the more of a reality it became in his mind. He thought of home for most of the ride and hardly realized their arrival into the forest. Light fog cast through the forest almost as if it were enchanted. Clearly, it had not been scourged with war.

While they located a small clearing, Edward looked at his surroundings. "Alf, William, Liam, and Charlie." The four men maneuvered their horses closer to him. "Stay on your guard, mates. Remember we are the front and I don't want any casualties. Understood?" Silently and solemnly everyone nodded. "Good. Charlie, Liam you take the first patrol, in three hours time William, Alfred, and myself will take the second. Report to Lieutenant Gyles first before leaving and see where he wants you to go." Liam nodded and guided his horse to the last known location of the Lieutenant with Charlie following close behind.

Edward climbed down from Frosty Queen and tied her to a low-lying branch before unpacking his equipment. He was quiet and continuously studied the landscape. There was great tension in the air, although they hadn't seen battle in a few days, the fear of being bombarded was still on their mind, especially in such a tight space.

William attempted to make a fire as Alfred and Edward began working on making a livable camp for their group. Taking down the camp a month ago seemed much more simple than putting one up. After struggling for a while, they finally had their waterproof tarps hanging over a few tree branches making a dry tent.

William finally had the fire going. The warmth was welcoming for once not many fires were in the trenches and many times the loss of feeling in the hands and feet came from the cold. Edward warmed up next to the fire as he pulled his journal out and began writing. He paused for a moment and flipped through the pages, noticing he had been journaling more and more since the Battle of Arras, more pages had been written during battle than out of battle. "What do you think, Ed?" William asked as Edward looked up.

"I think this war will go on for a little longer," he said, listening to their conversation as he wrote.

"Why do you say that?"

"Well, put it like this." He closed his journal and looked at both men in front of the fire. "We won a battle, yes. But do you really think the Germans are going to sit back with their tails between their legs? No. Of course they won't. They are going to retaliate. And when they do, we best be prepared. I fear they may attempt to come back to Arras, but that's why we're meeting them in Cambrai."

"But don't you think..."

"Thinking takes to long, Will. You take enough time to think and you end up with a hole in your head."

"Think less, shoot more," Alfred chuckled. Edward looked at him coldly but smirked.

"Although it sounds terrible, especially coming from Alf's lips, he is right. Just making sure you're shooting the Hun," Edward said. "Take a brief millisecond to think if you're shooting the right person."

Alfred twirled his ID disk between his fingers. Edward finally realized that he only did this when he was nervous, and lately his habit had worsened. It had started the night Edward reported George's death. Simply knowing someone so well had affected Alfred and Edward felt a little guilt and blamed himself for the habit.

"Alf, we'll be fine." Alfred meekly smiled and tucked his ID disk back into his shirt. For the next couple of hours they all sat in silence. Alfred wrote letters home while William sat carving something from a branch he found.

Edward listened. His eyes were shut and his head rested against a tree trunk. He was listening for anything out of the ordinary, and wanted to know every sound by the time they left the woods. When Liam and Charlie returned, he was the first to greet them.

"All is quiet."

"Not a soul. Except for us. I could use some food that's for sure."

"Get some rest and eat something, we'll be back in three hours," Edward pointed to the fire as he made his way to Frosty Queen. He looked at Alfred who finished his letter home and tucked it in his front chest pocket. After untying Frosty Queen, he mounted his horse and waited for Alfred and William to do the same. "Stay on your guard." Liam

nodded at Edward's order and made his way to the
fire.

Edward led his friends to where Lieutenant
Gyles stood at the edge of the camp. "We're ready
for patrol sir."

"Take to the East, patrol slowly and
cautiously. Report back immediately at the first
sight of something out of the ordinary. Do not
engage."

"Understood, sir," Edward said, saluting as
Lieutenant Gyles returned the gesture.

Nudging Frosty Queen in the ribs, Edward
led Alfred and William deeper into the woods. No
one said a word. The silence was so thick. Edward
rested his hand on the hilt of his sword. Edward
jumped at the sound of Blood Stream sneezing
causing the three men to break out in a moment of
laughter.

"Blood Stream got ya there, mate," Alfred
laughed as he patted his horses neck.

"He did," Edward looked over his shoulder.
When their laughter stopped, the fear crept back in.
The fear that had been present since the moment
they arrived at the forest. They barely knew their
surroundings. This was the perfect location for a
trap. No matter how many times Edward suppressed
the thought it kept emerging again, each time worse
than the last.

His thoughts stopped at the sound of twigs
breaking. Quickly he pulled back on the reins and
held one hand up. "What is-"

"Shut up," Edward demanded. Slowly he
scanned the horizon. Something rustled in the
bushes next to them. Unsheathing his sword he felt
his heart pounding in his throat, the feeling making
him near nauseous.

Suddenly, a German soldier charged from the bush and Edward sat on Frosty Queen frozen. The *crack* of gun made him jump. The German fell dead and Edward looked at William who held his pistol. "Go!" he ordered, turning Frosty Queen around. "Back to the camp, now!"

William and Alfred charged in front of Edward, who took a glance behind him. A few splinters of tree bark brushed his face as a bullet collided with a tree. "Germans!" he screamed. In the distance he could see the camp scrambling. He wondered if they could even hear him.

"Germans!" William and Alfred echoed. The second call seemed to reach them as men scrambled for their weapons. As they entered the camp just north, a shell exploded flinging dirt and splinters into the air.

"They have their bloody artillery?" Edward questioned as another shell exploded just south of the camp. "Get to Liam and Charlie!" Edward pointed to Alfred and William who kicked their horses in the direction of their camp. At the explosion of another shell, Edward watched in disbelief as three men were thrown into the air.

Frosty Queen reared catching Edward off guard as he fell from the saddle. He gasped for air as the wind was knocked from him. Frosty Queen whinnied as she reared again, and a close by shell explosion caused Edward to cower on the ground praying it didn't hit him. Wet dirt landed on his face. He sat up shaking as he spotted Frosty Queen lying on her side. He looked over his shoulder at the Germans who refused to advance as they bombarded the camp with shellfire. Another explosion brought him back. He crawled to Frosty Queen, pressed his hand to her side, and realized she was dead. "Queenie," he whimpered as another explosion shook his soul.

A passing soldier grabbed his arm and yanked him to his feet. "Get moving!" the man shouted. Edward locked his gaze on Frosty Queen as his fellow soldier dragged him away. Three more shells exploded around them. He fought back the tears as he realized he had been running. He separated from the soldier and made it back to his men, pinching the bridge of his nose trying to not show his sadness. "Retreat west. I saw Lieutenant Gyles gathering some men, find him and follow him." He glanced at Alfred who looked completely shell shocked. "Get a move on!"

"But sir, you need..."

"I'll find one, Will, go!"

William, Liam, and Charlie no longer hesitated and took off westward obeying orders. Alfred jumped down from Blood Stream.

"Go, Alf."

"I'm not leaving you behind," Alfred barked back over the sound of exploding shells. Men and horses scattered in the confusion as Edward and Alfred began running in the direction he ordered William, Liam, and Charlie. "Besides, lower targets are harder to hit." The sounds of shell explosions were softening. "I'm sorry about Frosty Queen," Alfred said as Edward held his hand up.

"Thank you, but not now," Edward ordered. "Just keep moving Alf." Edward paused to look over his shoulder.

The crack of a rifle made him rotate on his heals quickly. The world slowed as he watched Alfred fall. He looked to see the German cocking the bolt on his rifle. Angrily Edward pulled his pistol out and shot the German three times screaming. Alfred lay below Blood Stream holding his chest.

"Alf. Alf." Edward crumbled next to his friend. Grabbing him by the cheeks he turned his face toward him, his eyes were already dilated. "Alf," Edward mumbled his lower lip quivering. "Alf?" The bullet entry in his chest looked small but the blood loss was too great. Edward shook as he slowly stood. Numbly he lifted his friend off the ground and draped him over Blood Stream's back. "Come on, Blood Stream," he cried tugging at the reins.

He marched on, wiping away the tears that fell and glancing back from time to time secretly hoping Alfred really hadn't died. But he was reminded every time he looked back. As he approached the edge of the forest, he stopped Blood Stream and looked behind them panting.

The faint sounds of artillery continued, and Edward feared being followed. He looked at Alfred's body and pulled him down from Blood Stream, gently placing him in the dirt. He found an already prepared hole from an old shell explosion, placed his body in the pit and stared down at him. He knelt down and placed his hand on his friend's chest.

"Goodbye, my friend. Blood Stream will be in good hands. My promise to you is true." He said through tears. He took Alfred's helmet off placed it to the side and, remembering the letter he was writing home, reached in his front pocket and pulled out the blood stained piece of paper. "Take some rest, my friend. You fought well. I'm sorry," he cried.

The artillery fire grew louder, as if the Germans were on the move. Quickly he said his last goodbye and began burying Alfred in the old shell hole. When the hole was filled, he grabbed two broken branches and placed them in the shape of a cross, stepped back and took his helmet off, closing his eyes he no longer cared about the tears. "Goodbye, Alf."

For the third time that day his world slowed to a near stop. A loud pounding rang in his right ear as a shell exploded only a few feet from him sending him flying into a tree, knocking him out cold.

***

The bright sun woke him early a few days later. He looked around he wondered where he was. The room was comfortable and looked like a resort never touched by the war. He looked at the end table where his camera, journal, George's trumpet, and Alfred's blood stained letter rested. He pushed back the covers, examining himself he sighed as he still had his arms and legs.

The door opened, and he looked up. Adeline entered in a nurse's gown. "Sacré..." she whispered staring at him. Her voice sounded muffled and unclear. She stepped closer to him, placing her tray next to his bed. He glanced down nervously at the utensils on the tray unaware what any of them did. "How are you feeling, monsieur?" Her angelic voice was slightly distorted. He rubbed his right ear, but heard nothing, not even the muffle of his finger inside his ear.

"I can't hear out of my right ear," he said, frightened.

"I feared you would lose the hearing of the right ear," she sighed, walking to a table by the window. She leaned over and began writing. "Can you… um," she paused thinking for a moment. "Move right arm," she finished.

Slowly, he lifted his arm to ninety degrees and screamed out in pain before lowering it.

"Any higher? No?"

He shook his head rubbing his shoulder. "Where are my men? And Blood Stream?"

"Pardon, monsieur?" she walked over to him questioningly.

"The horse I was with, my Lieutenant, my unit, where is everyone?"

Adeline looked at him, not understanding everything he was asking. She shook her head having no answer for him, something which only made him more frustrated.

"I'll get a doctor, monsieur," she said.

Edward shook his head angrily. He didn't want to see a doctor, he wanted to see his friend's horse. He wanted to see Lieutenant Gyles and the others.

Adeline ignored his protests and left the room.

Chapter 15

30 June, 1917

I'm going home? I'm going home. I can't believe it even now as I write it. I've sat in this bed for almost a month. The doctor announced this morning I was unfit for battle. "A half-deaf man is just as useful as a dead man." I don't know whether I should be overzealous or insulted.

I fear my mother will no longer recognize me. I'll admit living in the trenches I've become colder. I thought death was so easy after George died. Watching others around me fall hardly affected me after that. It was easy to deal with. One day you were talking to someone, the next you were watching them being carried off by a medic. This war has taken so many lives. Alf's death nearly crippled me, though. It still kills me to even write of it. I knew him from the beginning and Lieutenant Gyles promised me he would make sure both Alf and I made it to the end.

I can't blame him for not being there, I was in charge. Alf's life was in my hands and I had been the one who failed him. He had so much trust. God, I should have never looked behind me, if I saw the rifle beforehand I could have shot him before he got to Alf. The only thing that gladdens me is I know he suffered none. He died quickly and that's all one could ask for in this war. There's so many 'what if's' going through my mind.

He is not completely innocent in his own death. I instructed him to go with William, but he was damn sure to stay with me after Frosty Queen… why am I losing everything? My horse I raised from a weanling. These damn Germans are taking everything from me, but as long as I stand my home will never be occupied. I can still see Frosty Queen lying there. Just like Alf, her death was instant never giving me a moment to say my farewell. But for a horse it was best that she passed with no pain. I've seen many a time a horse with a broken leg or back had to be put down on the farm. My father often did the job. He said it was best to do the job quickly and take the pain from the beast away.

1 July, 1917

I may have the opportunity of going to London now. Lieutenant Gyles, Charlie, William, and Liam came to visit me last night. It was awkward having them all standing on the left side of my bed. Lieutenant Gyles was the first to talk, while the other lads walked around my room finding spots to sit in. He told me that they were to be making their way for Cambrai in a few days. I was relieved to be lying in a bed. A day without cooties or bullets flying at my head was a good day for me. "But I'm not here to tell you what we're doing, the lads wanted to see how you were. I'm only here to ask you a question." I looked at him peculiarly, waiting for him to ask me if I was willing to go back and fight after the doctor declared me unfit. To be honest, I don't really want to go home, I'm going to worry more about those I know still here, especially Charlie, with no one to look after him. "I promised you when we left England, that I would protect you and… Alfred." Alf's death surly was getting to him. I didn't want to hear him mention Alf. His death still brought me to nausea. "I have a flat in London. You're still a fighter and that flame will never go out. What I'm proposing is, you upkeep my flat. On top of that, become an enlisting officer."

He told me he informed his sister she no longer needed to upkeep the flat, assuming I'd say yes. He also sent a petition letter to the branch in London demanding me a job as an enlisting agent. What was I going to say, no? I couldn't. I was practically railroaded.

Although I was looking forward to going home, deep down I really didn't want to. All I would do till this bloody war was over is farm and see my friends who turned of age ship off to come back tormented or not come back at all. I wasn't ready to see any more of my friends disappear, so I accepted Lieutenant Gyles offer. After that, we simply started sharing stories. Charlie asked about the trumpet on my bed stand. The room became quiet for a moment before I told him about George. When I did it seemed to have sparked a moment for us to honour the dead. We went around the room, each of us telling Charlie stories of those we had lost. Some before the war, some during. Most of my stories were about friends I had who lost their lives before I was old enough to enlist. Most of my friends lied about their age, got a scolding from their parents, and then left for the war. I know most have passed on already, but from time to time I hear about a few who are still fighting. I pray an entire generation doesn't get wiped out.

3 July, 1917

I lost my temper today, which I wouldn't have a problem with normally. Except this time it wasn't with a nurse who struggled to understand me, or a doctor who wouldn't bother listening to a damn word I had to say. Today I got frustrated with my men. Liam, Charlie, and William blessed me with another visit. I wasn't having the best of days as I had been informed that Blood Stream would be remaining with the company. How can I keep my promise to my friend if Blood Stream is not with me?

But that information was only the foundation of how frustrating this day became. When the lads came over to keep me company, it all sounded like noise. They all laughed and talked over each other. I heard nothing what Liam had to say since he was sitting on my right side and I simply blew up. I yelled and cursed and I think I threw my drinking glass across the room. What made me even angrier is that they stared at me with understanding. I don't want to be understood, my deafness has no bloody control over me and anyone who says otherwise can bloody bugger off.

6 July, 1917

It has been a few days since my last entry, for many reasons. So many things have been going on for my preparation to depart. I think today was the last time I will see Charlie. I pray he makes it through to the end. He's a strong kid. I see too much of myself when I first enlisted in him. He's innocent and unstained by war. The things he will endure will change him greatly, making him cold, callous, and intimidated by nothing. Which can be a good thing, but I fear for myself in a sense when I think upon this. I fear that I will not be able to blend with society again. I find myself still using every day trench slang for words no layperson would understand.

We sat in silence for a while, then he told me that the company were to be moving soon. He wishes he knew me better, but my kindness is all he could ask for. My kindness? I wasn't trying to be kind. I was simply making sure he didn't get smothered for looking weak. The men could be brutal, but for some unknown reason everyone looks... well I should say looked up to me. I'm simply now a shell of my former self, half deaf and unfit for battle.

What makes any man fit for battle? Back home, the examinations were practically a look over. If you looked well enough, you were in. Sometimes I think we just sent our young men to their deaths. Charlie continued on about how he'll look after Alf's horse. How he hopes to see me when all this hell is over. He took his time with me and his company was welcomed. It was good chatting with only one of them. Being able to hear someone talking to you is plenty nice. He gave me a small parcel of letters. Apparently, my entire company now knows I'm going home and wants me to send letters to their families homes from London. I smiled and nodded. I had no choice but to say yes.

When he left, and I was alone with my thoughts once more, I thought of London. I can't really say I'm going home. Yes, I'm returning to England, but I'm not going home to see my family. I'm more afraid of any battle in the trench or cootie than facing my mother. Would she recognize me? I'm not the same son I was when I left. I've reminded myself time after time, I think I've written it a hundred times in this journal. Those that I have killed, do I have remorse? I don't feel that I do. For I know none I have killed. Wilhelm was the only German I met that seemed human, and fear flowed from him. If I had shot him that day, it may have been different. Murder, I'd say. Secretly I contemplated letting him go.

Another doctor just left. I'm sick and tired of these doctors. He raised my arm, and surprisingly I can now raise it further than ninety degrees. He said I was in good health and should be leaving soon. Honestly, I'm ready to go. Although I want to return to war, I'm ready to leave France behind me. He said it shouldn't be too long now. And now I'm alone in this room. Not simply left alone, but I feel loneliness inside me. The world is quiet here. The outside looks calm, there are no scars of war here. I came to France with everything and now I leave with nothing, nothing except my memories. I'll send a letter home to my mother when I arrive in London. I miss them all. I think about them daily. George, Alf, Frosty Queen, Jack, all of them. They are more than friends when you climb into those trenches. Those with you become your family. It is difficult when one of those family members passes. But it becomes the most difficult when you realize that you'll be the only one leaving the trench out of all of them. You wonder if they secretly hate you for leaving? You wonder if they will make it out when the war ends or, maybe find themselves in

your situation. Sitting in a hospital waiting…just
waiting.

-   Lance Corporal Edward Jacob Poole

Chapter 16

Edward closed his eyes and listened to the rhythmic click-clack of the tracks beneath the train. He was exhausted from the war, recovering, and most recently traveling all day. He left Amiens early that morning, and crossing the channel by ship that morning was the hardest part. He felt sick the entire crossing, the waves were large and rough. Now he tried relaxing, knowing he'd be in London shortly. He opened his journal again reading the address Lieutenant Gyles had given him. The sliding door to his cabin opened, but he hadn't heard it. "Ticket please," the train guard called out.

"Excuse me?"

"Ticket?" Edward nodded and reached in his pocket, handing the man his ticket. "Thank you," the older man said before punching a hole in it. He handed Edward the ticket once more and left him to listen to the train. Edward thought of taking a shower and sleeping in a bed without worrying about doctors interrupting his rest. He laughed at the thought of how many visits he received a day, making sure he was comfortable. He was glad that part of life was over. Suddenly, the door to his cabin opened again. He found himself staring at a pair of women's black heels. Slowly, he looked up.

"May I join you?" a thin brunette asked. She wore a blue summer dress that frilled at the bottom and a matching hat. She seemed to love the color blue. Even her eyes were blue. Edward found himself staring wordlessly at her pale complexion. "Sir?"

"Please," he cleared his throat gesturing to the bench across from him, then returned his attention to the sounds of the train. Closing his eyes, he leaned back in his seat.

"You seem to be going the opposite direction to the war," the new arrival said, her voice a little louder than the noise that came from the train. Edward looked up, his facial expression indicating he'd heard nothing of what she said, causing her to repeat herself.

"I've served my time," he answered. His uniform was clean and comfortable for once, she obviously made the comment on seeing him fully garbed. "I'm considered lucky."

"Are you?"

"Honestly, I don't know. I wonder if I'm lucky? I return to England alone, so I don't think so."

"You live in London?"

"For the time being. If I were to go home, I'd sit on this train for an extra two hours," he chuckled.

Edward looked her over, studying her, wondering what was going on in her mind. She was rather pretty, he guessed her age to be around twenty. He noticed her soft face studying him back.

"You don't look to be sick or injured? What happened?" She was forward, too. "Pardon, how rude of myself."

"You're simply curious, it's fine. And what happened you ask? Well, I'll tell you." He hardly knew her yet felt so natural around her. She wasn't bossy like Christine had been, or uninterested like Adeline. "I'm deaf in one ear," he said pointing to his right ear.

"Completely?"

"Completely." He chuckled at the sound of surprise in her voice. "It's a tale I would rather not talk about today, but long story short, I was nearly killed by shrapnel. Instead of it taking my life, it took my hearing in one ear."

When she received her answer, the girl seemed content and focused her attention on the window. Edward closed his eyes, rested his chin to his chest, and focused on the sounds of the train again.

"Do you have a map?" Edward looked up. The silence of the train stopped was perfect he could hear her clearly.

"I do not, but I'll pick one up when we arrive in London."

"Have you ever been to London?"

"Of course, once, but that was when I was younger. I went with my father to get some things for the farm. I don't remember much."

"Well it has changed quite a bit. Louder, brighter." Edward nodded politely as the train pulled out of the station. "I would be happy to show you around, look at some of the sights."

"You know London well, apparently."

"Well, I moved there with my family four or five years ago. And seeing you in uniform…" she paused while Edward felt warm in the face, unaware he was turning a light shade of red. "You remind me of when my brother left for France." His smile faded. She giggled on seeing the transformation in his face. "This bloody war," she sighed.

"Pardon me for asking, is your brother still alive."

"I hope so," she answered. She looked melancholy. "He just recently left, or what feels like recently. I go down to Kent every week to pick up supplies for my family's shop, while at the same time hoping to see my brother get off one of the ships from France."

Edward listened to her talk about her brother for a while. He learned that he was a few years older than him, and not skilled to be a soldier. According to this woman. He learned all about her, except one important detail, her name.

"Forgive me," he interrupted. She looked at him politely and calmly a warm smile on my face. "Our conversation has been most enjoyable, however there is one thing we have yet to clear up."

"And what would that be sir?"

"Your name." She blushed and covered her mouth.

"Vera Hood. And you are?"

"Lance Corporal Edward Poole. Nice to make your acquaintance, Miss Hood," he said shaking her hand.

"Please, I'm only known as Vera amongst my friends," she said. Edward hardly realized the train was pulling into Paddington. "Looks like we've arrived, Lance Corporal," she smirked, rising from her seat.

Edward looked out the window seeing the busy train station before him. People moved around each other like a swarm of angry ants, soldiers and families hugged and waved goodbye, while others shouted at each other over the deafening sounds of the crowd. Edward stood and grabbed his bag from above before following after Vera. "Where is it that you're going?" she asked as they stepped off the train. Edward looked at her, hearing nothing that came from her lips. The train station was too loud.

"I can't hear you," he screamed as she put her hand up.

"You don't have to scream," she instructed, but he still could not hear her. He became frustrated and agitated.

"Bloody hell, it's too loud. All these poodlefakers in the bumf," he said, unaware he'd begun cursing in frustration. He looked around the train station, the flood of sound conjoined into one. His mind felt lost and the frustration he felt the day he threw his drinking glass with his friends in the room came rushing back. He caught a glimpse of Vera, she looked shocked but he couldn't focus on her. The noise was already giving him a headache.

"Come with me," she snapped grabbing his upper arm, she began walking for the exit. He could tell she was upset, was it something he did or said? He tried ignoring the whistles of trains and shouting of people. When they left the station and entered the streets, the sound was more tolerable, but not by much. "Better?" she asked standing to his right.

"What did you say?" he asked again. She studied him he watched her as she slowly walked in front of him and stood to his left.

"I said is that better?"

"A little. I wasn't... expecting it to be that loud."

"That's the city for you." She didn't look too happy.

"Did I by chance say something that may have upset you?"

"Now you don't remember what you even said."

He shook his head innocently.

"Your language is strong, Mr. Poole," she said curtly. He quickly realized the offence he'd committed. Surprisingly, he wasn't at all apologetic for what he said. It was an everyday word to him.

"I'm sorry for my loose tongue, Vera," he said as kindly as he could. She simply nodded, her facial expression never changing giving him no form of assurance.

"Do you have an address?" she asked as Edward quickly took out his journal. He handed the book to her and showed her where Lieutenant Gyles had written his home address. "That's not too far from here. It's a few blocks north of Piccadilly." She gave him his journal back, he put it back in his back pocket. "Righto, this way," she instructed before walking away from him.

He looked around momentarily before following after her. They walked in silence for a few streets. Edward wondered what he could talk about while he took the sights of the city in. On nearly every corner stood a man in uniform trying to recruit another soldier. They stopped at the corner of a busy street waiting to cross.

"Ah, soldier on your way to the front?" an enlister asked Edward. Luckily the man was standing close to Edward's left ear. He caught every word. Edward looked at the older man briefly.

"No, sir, I'm home to stay."

"Home? But look at you, you're healthy and strong."

"And deaf," he said. The recruiter began laughing, but Edward looked at him with a serious glance.

"If you were deaf, we wouldn't be conversing right now. Is that your excuse for why you aren't fighting, lad?" Edward started to become irritated with the man. "You clearly are ready in that uniform to fight for King and Country."

"I've done my time fighting for King and Country. Now bugger off."

"He lost his hearing in his right ear from shrapnel, sir," Vera snapped as the recruiter took a small step back.

"Idiot, bastard," Edward grumbled as the traffic changed and they crossed the street leaving the recruiter behind them. Vera smirked as they continued southward. After a good thirty-minute walk, they finally reached where Edward would be lodging. He wondered how long he would remain in London, how much longer the war would go on, and how long he would be recruiting people.

"This is you," Vera said pointing to the brick building before them.

"I guessed that," he smiled. "Well Vera, it was grand meeting you and I thank you very much for helping me around."

"It was my pleasure." They stood awkwardly for a moment.

"Well-" they both started before laughing.

"You first," Vera smiled.

"Well, I was going to ask. Could I possibly see you again?" Vera looked surprised at his offer.

Edward had an innocent look about him, although that innocence had been taken by the war.

"See me how?" she asked tilting her head back a little.

"Well," he coughed. He wondered why he felt so nervous. "What are you doing tomorrow night?"

"Tomorrow night?"

"It is Friday tomorrow, right?" Edward asked.

"Nothing at the moment, why?"

"Would you like to go dancing?"

"Where exactly?" Edward stopped and thought a bit. He knew nothing of London, and became silent. She smiled as he began to turn red again. "Tell ya what, I'll stop by around half four tomorrow, and I'll show ya around. Then we can go dancing." Edward smiled.

"Meet me here, then?" he asked pointing to the ground.

"Now, if you'll excuse me, Edward, I really must be going." He nodded and watched her walk off down the road; her brunette curls bobbing as she walked. He smiled and made his way into the flat building. Climbing the stairs to the fourth floor, he walked down the hall to the last door on the left. There, he found a letter taped to the door.

"Dear Mr. Poole, my brother informed me that you'll be staying here for a while, and you are more than welcome to stay as long as you need to. I've left the key to the flat with your neighbor simply ask them for it. Didn't want to leave it under the mat. Sincerely, Lucy Gyles."

He read the letter out loud before placing his bag down. After knocking on the neighbor's door he waited. A little boy no older than six opened the door and looked up at him.

"Are you my papa?" the boy asked as Edward chuckled and shook his head.

"I'm sorry there," a woman appeared at the door. "You must be my temporary neighbor, Miss Gyles was telling me about." Edward silently nodded. "Said you were a friend of her brother's."

"Actually he was my lieutenant," Edward answered.

"And I'm guessing you're enjoying yourself here."

"Chuffed to bits, to be honest," he answered. "I was too young to remember the last time I was in London."

"Well, welcome. And if you need anything, I'm nearly always home," she smiled.

"Thank you, Mrs...."

"Stewart," she smiled. "Kelly Stewart."

"Nice to meet you, Mrs. Stewart. I'm Edward," he said, shaking her hand.

"Are you sure you're not my papa?" Edward laughed and knelt next to the boy.

"I'm sure," he said. The boy looked disappointed and ran back into the flat.

Mrs. Stewart handed him the key and Edward said his farewell before entering his flat. It was a standard one-bedroom flat, the perfect size for one person, and could comfortably fit two people. The floors were an old rustic wood, and the windows thick and lightly frosted. Clearly, Lieutenant Gyles liked his privacy.

Edward placed his bag in the bedroom and sat down in one of the club chairs. He looked at the radio that rested on the floor to ceiling bookshelf. Nearly every shelf was full with books. The smell of fresh paint filled his nostrils. He leaned his head back and closed his eyes.

He was woken to the sound of someone knocking on his door. Standing up, he looked around wondering how long he had been resting. He unlocked the door and found a man twice his age standing there in full uniform. "Lance Corporal Poole?" the man asked saluting as Edward returned the salute.

"Yes, and you are?"

"Private Olsten," the man answered. "May I come in?" Edward stepped back, allowing the man to enter. He closed the door and followed the man into the living quarters of the flat. "You probably know the reason for my visit, but I'll still tell you anyways." The man sat down in one of the club chairs. "I'm here to guide you around the city, especially to the recruitment office. It's not too far from here."

"I was told that I wouldn't be starting until tomorrow."

"And that is correct, but it would be wiser to show you where everything is before we set you out on the streets to recruit. It has also been brought to my attention that you are deaf in the right ear?"

"Correct, shrapnel explosion," he answered before Olsten could ask how.

"Very well, I shall be on your left side the entire time. And if at anytime you cannot hear me, please inform me," Olsten sighed standing up. "Shall we leave?"

Edward was ready to take a nap instead of walking around the city, but it seemed he didn't have much of a choice. He extended his hand to the door telling the older man to lead on. "Very well, let's go," the man smiled as they left the flat.

Chapter 17

Edward stood in the center of Piccadilly Circus, the sounds of automobiles, horses, and people were bothering him. He remained calm and looked at any man who seemed fitting. He'd approach and discuss the war with him, although he barely heard what the other said. Most of the men ignored him. He understood their reasons. Although he hadn't heard all the excuses, he knew what the real excuse was. Fear. Fear that you'd end up losing your head and never returning.

Although Edward wondered why so many felt that way. He remembered the excitement he felt when he finally was allowed to enlist. He wondered why the people in the city did not feel the same way. After leaving France and seeing what he saw he refused to blame no one for not wanting to go into that hell. He realized simply talking to the men got him no responses, so he became creative. "The war will be over soon, and with you fighting it'll be over sooner," he said to one man who simply laughed and continued walking. "Don't cower behind your lass, be a man," he said to another who looked at him angrily before moving on. He spent most of the morning yelling at the men who looked able-bodied and strong enough to fight. He was finally successful in stopping one young man. He was Edward's height and aged twenty. The man said something in Edward's right ear but he couldn't hear him. "Can you stand on my left, mate?" The man obliged and positioned to Edward's left.

"I'll sign up," the man repeated. "I've got nothing here anyways."

"I'm sure that's not true." But the man's stoney expression never changed.

Edward began discussing with the man all the questions he remembered from his so-called training the day before. He looked over the man and noticed something white in his hand, but ignored it and continued with his questions. After the man looked for certain he was ready, Edward walked with him back to the recruitment office.

Private Olsten sat at the desk and began clapping as Edward brought his first recruit into the room. Edward was unsure if the private was being sarcastic or not. As Edward turned to leave and return to his post, he watched as the man placed a white feather on the desk. Private Olsten then discarded the feather.

Edward returned to Piccadilly Circus where he spent the rest of the day calling out. By the end of the day, his throat was hoarse. He only signed two men up, and started to become suspicious of this white feather when he noticed both men had been holding one. He then let the thoughts of the feather and of his long day recess in the back of his mind as he walked home. He began thinking of Vera, and wondered where they would go that evening.

When he got home he quickly changed out of his uniform and into civilian clothing, stopping in front of the mirror to take a long gander at himself. It had been nearly a year since he'd worn civilian clothing, and he felt oddly uncomfortable.

With his officers jacket in his hand he reached into the pocket and pulled out the silver war badge. He looked at the pin for a moment reading the inscription out loud. "For King and Empire. Services Rendered." Pinning it to his lapel, he looked back at his reflection, he felt a strong source of pride when looking at the pin. Soon his focus moved from his reflection to the trumpet that rested on his end table. He turned around and looked at the trumpet and letter he took from his friends. He nodded in respect before looking at his pocket watch. Satisfied, he left his flat to wait for Vera on the street. At half four she arrived, putting a small smile on Edward's face.

"How long have you been standing out here?"

"Not long at all," he lied. She took his left arm and the two began walking down the street. "I was thinking maybe we should get something to eat first before we go out dancing for a little."

"A little?"

Vera looked up at him her blue eyes studying him.

"You do realize there is a curfew right?" she asked. He chuckled, pretending he knew all about it. "Many get mighty suspicious of people out past seven, especially the women. Last week I saw a girl maybe seventeen get stopped outside my flat for being out too late. She was just crossing the road from her grandmother's flat across the way. This world is going to hell, Edward."

"This isn't hell, Vera," he sighed. She respectfully became quiet.

They walked in silence for a few blocks. Edward's mind drifted it was hard seeing so many people acting like nothing was going on. Living their lives as if their brothers, their sons and husbands weren't dying.

They arrived at the restaurant, a fancy place he knew he wasn't able to afford. He looked at Vera. "Here?" he asked. She could see it in his eyes he was hiding nothing.

"It's okay. I'll pay."

"No."

"Oh don't be such a traditionalist. You invited me out, but let me take care of the bill. Plus it's one of the few places in London you'll be able to hear a conversation in." They walked up to the podium where the hostess stood patiently.

"Two?" Vera and Edward nodded as the woman smiled, picking up two menus. "Right this way."

They walked behind her, Vera leading Edward. They were placed in the corner right next to the window overlooking the street below. By now it had grown quiet outside, only a few people walked here and there. The city was getting quieter and readying for curfew. He looked to Vera, his hands felt clammy as they shook. His mouth felt dry and suddenly he had a strong urge to smoke. Pulling a fag out, he lit it and inhaled deeply letting the smoke fill his lungs before he blew out.

"So where do you come from?" she asked, unbothered by him smoking. He hardly spoke of home, but it wasn't about the war so he smiled and relaxed a little.

"Bourne, like I said, two hours north," he smiled.

"I remember."

"And yourself?"

"And myself what?"

"Where are you from?"

"Here."

"No you're not," Edward laughed. She looked at him funny. "You don't sound it."

"How would a little country boy like yourself know where I'm from?" Vera leaned forward with a smile, her elbows on the table. "You told me you've only been to London once, are you an expert of English accents?"

"No, but I do know a Norfolk tongue when I hear one. A few of my comrades were from there." Vera looked at him surprised and sat back in her seat. She squinted a little, but her smile gave her away.

"Alright, I'll give you that one. You can obviously tell where I'm from. But you can't tell me why I came to London."

"I can guess," he pointed at her as the waiter came by.

"Can I get you two started off with something to drink?" the man asked, placing a small basket of bread between them.

"I'm fine with some water," Edward said politely before looking back to Vera.

"Oh that's it?" Vera pouted. Edward looked at her slightly crossed. "Bottle of your finest champagne and two glasses." She smiled at the waiter who nodded and left.

"Vera we can't afford champagne."

"You may not be able to, but I told you not to worry."

But he did worry. He worried quite a bit.

"Vera..."

"Not another word about it," she smiled.

Edward sighed and sat back. "You've been at war for how long?"

"Nearly a year."

"And how does it feel to wear normal clothing for once?"

"Incredibly odd," he said with no hesitation. "I took a long gander at myself in the mirror before meeting you downstairs. I almost wished to be in my uniform."

"You were in your uniform all day, I'm sure you want some freedom from it."

"What I want is this damned war to be done with," he said bitterly. A few older couples looked at his table. "Sending our friends to fight a war fit for governments. Damn blokes can't do anything right." Vera sat quietly as Edward ranted on. "I lost two of my best friends to this damn war."

"Edward," Vera whispered as he looked up. He forgot where he was momentarily. Thinking of George and Alfred seemed to have taken him back to France. She seemed to have no problems with most of his aggravation, except that of the stronger language.

"Sorry," he apologized before realizing other tables had heard him. The waiter returned with the champagne and poured Vera's glass then Edward's. She held her champagne flute up and looked Edward dead in the eyes.

"To our heroes. Those that have passed, and those lucky enough to come home," she said as Edward raised his glass to hers.

"Well said." He took a sip and returned his attention to the menu. He was debating between the lamb or the duck.

"Did you know an Edmund Hood?" Vera asked, causing him to look up.

"A few more minutes?" the waiter asked as they both shook their heads. Vera ordered the duck and Edward ordered the lamb. When the waiter left, he returned his attention to her previous question.

"No, the name doesn't seem that familiar. Is that your brother?"

She nodded.

"It is. And I told you it wasn't that too long ago that he enlisted." Edward nodded. She seemed to change in that moment. The sweet innocent seeming girl he met on the train seemed to melt into sorrow. "I worry about him awfully much. I was hoping you knew him."

"Well, it depends on the branch. I was apart of the Calvary. The 4th Queen's Own Hussars."

"I wouldn't know what branch he was with. The last letter I received from him was maybe a month ago."

"Well, keep in mind some of our letters never make it home. With the military police checking what we write some get intercepted. So maybe your brother has written some letters that the military doesn't want your family reading."

"Like what."

"I'd rather not say," he paused taking a sip of champagne. "This war is dark and dreadful."

"Then help me understand," Vera sighed.

Edward sat silently for a moment looking at her. She was so innocent in all of this. He questioned if he was willing to strip the innocence from her. He thought on it some more, trying to find a delicate way of breaking the war to her.

"Very well," he sighed, finishing his glass of champagne in one big gulp before pouring another. "If this is really what you want to hear." He paused waiting for her to protest, but her protest never came. He took a deep breath and let out another sigh. "You say this world is going to hell and indeed it is. But what you and most who haven't seen the war don't understand what hell is. Hell is seeing the land being ripped apart by shrapnel explosions. Trees splitting and splintering killing anyone in their path, men dying all around you and having no choice but to ignore it. While others try to injure themselves by shooting themselves to get discharged or deliberately looking over the top of the trench for a German to shoot them in the head to escape this world for the next. Imagine one friend slowly dying by himself in a pit made by one of those shrapnel shells. Imagine finding him looking scared, begging you to talk of home to forget his pain."

"Is that when you lost your hearing?"

"No. George was the first encounter I had with death." Edward sat for the next half hour over dinner telling Vera anything he wanted about the war. His opinions on what was happening and the friends he had lost. He told her his fears for the men he was enlisting, and that he felt a regret deep inside him. He felt the need to hold off on the day they were ambushed in the woods, but in the heat of the moment it simply came out.

"So you were all scrambled?"

"Completely. I felt empty and drained. We had been fighting for a month as it was. And it hadn't helped that I just lost the horse that I raised since she was born."

The melancholy conversation didn't affect him as much as he thought it would. He almost felt relieved. Someone was willing to listen to his story. "This was the day I lost my hearing, actually." Vera leaned a little closer she looked captivated by his story, as if it was that, a story. "When I reached my men, I instructed them to go find the Lieutenant. Three of them left, my friend Alf, refused to leave my side. Taking the reins of his horse Blood Stream, he and I began making our retreat. We were getting further away from the artillery fire and I looked over my shoulder."

Edward stopped talking. He could still hear the gunshot as if it happened right then and there. He could still see Alfred's dilated pupils.

Vera was silent, he could see in her eyes she wanted to know more. He could also see the respect she held for him preventing her from pushing him into giving her more information. Taking a deep breath, he took a sip of champagne and continued. "That's when I heard the rifle fire. When I turned around, Alf was dead and that bloody Jerry was readying to shoot me. I took his life instead."

"And what happened to your hearing?"

"I lost it shortly after burying Alf. An explosion threw me into a tree and I went out cold. When I woke, I was in Amiens in a soldier hospital, unable to hear from my right ear." He finished the last of his lamb and sat back. He felt as if a weight had been lifted off his shoulders. For some unknown reason, he found telling Vera his story to be simple and easy.

When dinner had finished and Edward finally let Vera pay, they left and Vera took Edward to the nearest dance hall. It wasn't too crowded and most of the men there were in uniform, a sure sign they were enjoying their last days of freedom before either leaving for the first time or returning to hell. Edward had great fun the rest of the night, dancing with Vera. They hardly spoke inside the hall since Edward could barely hear her. They mostly danced to ragtime in a one-step. At eight, Edward and Vera left the dance hall. Edward was quiet as he listened to Vera talk.

"And this one time," she laughed, "Edmund gave the commissioner Mrs. Bride's order and the commissioner hers." Edward laughed as she continued. "Oh, Mrs. Bride was not happy when she returned with shaving cream and razors. She wasn't the nicest of people and Edmund is one of those types who doesn't know when to stop talking. When he took her things back he apologized, as rightfully he should have, but then he said-" Vera cleared her throat and in a deeper tone almost mocking her brother, said, "Well, Mrs. Bride, seeing the hairs on your chin I thought you finally realized and bought the essential things you needed."

"I bet that went over well."

"It most certainly did not. Papa came in and pulled Edmund away while trying to calm Mrs. Bride down. Let's just say after that Edmund remained in the storage closest from then on."

They stopped outside Edward's flat. "I had a good-" Vera began, but before she could finish, Edward leaned forward, grabbed the back of her neck and kissed her. They lingered in the kiss for a while the tension in their bodies loosened and a burning fire ignited deep within Edward.

"Tomorrow?" he whispered as their lips finally separated. Vera said nothing, only nodded shyly.

Edward smiled, his face so close to hers he felt her breath on his neck. "Tomorrow," he whispered again, kissing her forehead.

He stepped back, she looked shocked but the small smile on her face gave her away. Grabbing his key out of his pocket he turned to the door. Vera grabbed his wrist and when he turned, she leaned in for another kiss. The second one was just as long as the first. Vera left him standing on the street a wide dumb smile on his face. When she turned the corner he finally went inside.

***

Days turned to weeks, weeks then turned to months, and Edward was spending most of his nights with Vera. Often she would arrive in Piccadilly Circus around lunch and they would grab something quick to eat. She'd even allow him to pay from time to time. Edward was happy, he didn't think it was possible, but he was slowly forgetting his life at war. He remembered his friends he lost deep down, but the effects of the losses were bothering him less. From time to time, he'd read Alfred's letter home before tucking it back in the pocket Bible he read in the trenches. George's trumpet rested on the counter in his kitchen, giving a place to honor his other friend. He placed them in places he wouldn't forget them.

He continued to work recruiting men who looked healthy and strong. Some came empty handed, others came with white feathers. He never asked what the feathers meant. He simply did his duty. He met with Vera almost every day. He was falling in love, and he thought she was too. She made him happy. He wanted to stay with her even after the war ended. They walked by the river at night, and sometimes danced too. Edward was finally living a normal life. He stopped thinking about the past and looked to the future. He lived with being deaf, and concentrated on listening more with his good ear. It was hard at times, but he worked hard to listen. He was getting better at focusing on one person. He didn't do it perfectly, but he tried.

On New Year's Eve, Edward cooked for Vera in his flat. They had a quiet evening, just the two of them. Vera read her brother's letter out loud. "Send my love home, Vera. Tell Mum and Dad not to worry we're doing our duty here and we should be done soon. I can feel it. This is going to be a good year, with love. Edmund."

"He seems to be writing you more and more."

"He is. But something deep down still worries me."

"Vera, you have nothing to worry about," he said, unsure himself. He knew he was lying, but he wanted to cheer her up. "I mean from what he writes, he isn't in the worst part, he's pretty cushy if you ask me."

"Cushy?"

"Safe and comfortable. He's writing to you a lot, which tells me he isn't on the front lines." Vera sighed and looked at her brother's letter again. "Come on, Vera," he sighed prying it from her hands. "It's New Year's Eve, have a glass of champagne and forget the war for a little." He handed her a glass and sat next to her. He grabbed her free hand and looked into her eyes. Besides, I feel your brother is right. The war is ending. I can feel it deep down. This is the year, believe you me."

"I'll believe it when Big Ben triumphantly rings the bells again."

Edward chuckled and took a drink. They sat in silence all the way until midnight of New Year's Day. Vera gave him a kiss, finished her champagne, and collected her things. "Don't go," he sighed leaning back.

"My parents…"

"Vera, it's well past curfew anyways. Your parents will understand. Tell them you were at a friend's house." She stood before the door, considering her options. "Come on, Vera," he smiled without moving from his spot at the table.

"All right, then," she said and moved back to her place.

***

As the months carried on, Edward began doubting more and more what he had said to Vera on New Year's about the war ending soon. By summer, he was standing numbly in Piccadilly Circus trying to get any new recruits. His job had become harder and harder. Some days, he simply wanted to stay in bed with Vera and sleep the morning away.

But they both had work to do.

Chapter 18

Edward found himself waking next to Vera as the early autumn sun came through the window. She looked peaceful wrapped in nothing but the bed sheets. He looked to the chair across the room where his union suit hung. Glancing back at Vera, he slowly climbed out of bed stark naked and tiptoed across the room. The floorboard creaked beneath him and he stopped as Vera let a soft whimper out. He turned and looked at her, her pale arm fishing the covers for him. He stood silently for a minute until she stopped fishing and rolled away from him. He let out a soundless sigh as he continued for his union suit.

"Come back to bed, and warm me," she mumbled. He stopped, quickly grabbed the suit and shyly covered himself. Turning, he saw Vera smiling at him using the bed sheets as cover. "Come on Soldier, and leave the under garments. That's an order," she smiled devilishly.

"Vera it's…"

"It's Sunday, I thought you took Sunday's off?" she pouted.

"But we have service."

"We can go to a later service," she smirked. She was very convincing.

He smiled, threw the union suit back on the armrest and returned to bed. They spent the entire morning writhing beneath the sheets and went to the noon service instead.

Not having eaten anything all morning, Edward was starving when they got out of the church. They went to a close-by pub and took a table. The place was rather quiet, with a few patrons scattered throughout the building. At the bar, two men sat and Edward could hear their small debate about enlisting since they sat to his left and weren't that far from their table.

"Do you want-" He held his finger up making Vera silent while he listened.

"You know why we can't. The army doesn't take flat foot."

"We know that, but we don't have to tell them."

"Edward, it's Sunday," Vera sighed pulling his attention from the conversation at the bar. "You don't work on Sunday's and besides, they aren't fit."

"I help whoever wants to go."

"No man wants to march to their death."

"They aren't marching to their death, Vera."

"Why? Because you know exactly where they will be sent?"

"No, but…"

"Stop," she interrupted him by grabbing him by the hand and looking at him sweetly.

"Very well."

They ordered a small lunch and sat talking about what happened the past week. Edward spoke of what he read in the papers, while Vera talked about fashion. Although neither truly cared about the other's subject, they listened. After they finished eating, Vera excused herself for the toilet while Edward swore to pay. When she was gone, he made a dash to the bar, sitting next to the taller of the two men.

"So you two are interested in the war?" he asked. He took a gander and realized they were identical twins; they looked to be at the age of twenty-three. The blonde boys looked at Edward slightly agitated.

"You can say that for my brother," the one Edward sat next to pointed to the other.

"Lance Corporal Edward Jacob Poole, at your service," he said quickly shaking each of their hands.

"Tommy Atkins," the one next to Edward said.

"Jacob Atkins," the other said before drinking from his beer.

"What makes you remain behind? Especially a Lance Corporal?" Tommy asked as Edward reached for his lapel. He looked down and realized he left his Silver War Badge in his flat.

"Injured in battle," he answered. "Look I don't have much time, if you really are interested come see me in Piccadilly tomorrow. We'll talk then," he whispered looking over his shoulder as he noticed Vera leaving the toilets. He stood up made his way to the barmaid and paid for their lunch before nodding to the twins. Vera greeted him with a kiss and the two left.

They strolled down the street. Vera hung on his arm, her head leaning against him. "I love you, Vera," he said.

She stopped walking and looked at him blankly for a moment.

"I love you too," she smiled, taking him by the hand. Her face went from doting and love filled to slightly worried. "What time is it?"

Edward paused reaching into his pocket and pulled his watch out.

"Half three, why?" he asked looking at the little clock.

"Great."

"What?"

"I have to go."

"Vera," he laughed tugging her back to him.

"No, Edward. I really have to go. I have to pick up a few things for the shop. I'll meet you for dinner at five."

"You promise?"

She stood on her tiptoes kissing him.

"I promise," she answered as he released his grip and let her go. He watched as she slowly walked down the street, never once looking back.

When she was out of sight, he turned and made his way to the park. As he strolled through the green expanse, he contemplated how to allow the twins he met earlier to sign up.

He took a seat at a bench and simply stared blankly at the people who strolled the park that Sunday. Couples young and old, women by themselves, and men too. The world looked to be at peace. No one acted as if a war was going on. Everyone pretended that life was normal. Edward even believed that thought to be true from time to time. Vera had taken him away from the thoughts of the early days at war. He was starting to forget. Edward had been back in England for a little over a year, and already he felt just like another citizen looked. Worried only about what he would wear and where he would take Vera. The war was simply a way to finance his life. Getting paid to sign a few lads up and move on with his day.

Edward was deep in his thoughts when he finally realized he wasn't alone. He looked to his left and noticed a young girl about seventeen sitting on the bench. She sat looking at the people as he had been. "It's a glorious Sunday isn't it?"

"It's sunny for once," he chuckled leaning back.

"I love Sundays like this."

Edward really wasn't in a mood to talk so he let her speak on.

"My man left for the war four months ago."

"Oh... I'm sorry to hear that," he said quietly as she looked at him.

"Why? He's doing his duty," she said. Edward could tell she was judging him, but he remained silent. "How old are you?" she asked squinting her eyes.

"Nineteen, ma'am." He looked at her peculiarly.

"Nineteen and still comfortable at home while your fellow Englishman fights?"

For some reason no matter how much he wanted to protest, something kept him silent. "You're probably like most boys here, comfortable with your woman afraid to go and be a man," she said standing. "I can't convince you. You're in charge of your own life. But just know that while you sit back and relax, there's others fighting for you." She said opening his jacket placing something in the inside pocket.

Edward sat angry as he watched her walk away. He wondered what kept him silent. He reached in his inside pocket and pulled a white feather out. He stared at the feather numbly and looked back to where the woman was. He focused back on the feather, a feeling of guilt and embarrassment settling down deep inside him.

For some reason, he felt guilty for nearly forgetting about the war. He started wondering how many of the men he signed up were still alive. Seeing the white feather, he understood what it meant. Those that had it when they signed up must have felt the same guilt he did. The white feather was a stigma of being a coward. He was angry not only with himself for leaving his Silver War Badge back at the flat but now the girl who presented the feather to him. She had not known him, or what he had been through, but deep down he longed to return to fight with those of his friends that remained.

All through the rest of the day he contemplated the white feather. Even when it wasn't in sight he thought about it. He barely heard a word Vera said to him from dinner through the rest of the evening. He didn't want to burden her with his thoughts, so he simply listened to her. He loved her presence, but now thought he needed to do more, that he needed to fight for her.

Vera left his flat a little past seven before curfew was enacted. When he was alone, he returned to the feather. He wondered why he was obsessing over it. As he prepared himself for bed, he realized the morning would bring a new day and the deal with the feather would be behind him.

But when he woke the next day, the feeling of being branded a coward had not left him. He felt even more guilty than he did the day before, as if it was a poison eating at him.

When he stood in Piccadilly trying to enlist other men, he seemed distracted. The Atkins twins showed up that very afternoon. Jacob spoke mostly, and Tommy agreed from time to time. "I'm not going to be the ones forcing you to sign. You need to be a hundred percent sure you want to do this."

Edward could see that Tommy didn't want to go.

"We're sure, that is if you can get us in," Tommy spoke up, his voice cracking a little. Jacob nodded with a big excited smile.

"Very well, follow me," he instructed. Silently they walked onward. Edward knew of another recruitment office linked to his regiment, but it was quite a walk. As they walked down the street, he instructed them on what to tell the recruiters and what not to. Tommy and Jacob never asked where they were going, and half an hour of walking later they arrived at the recruitment office. The three men walked in; there was hardly anyone inside.

"I've brought two more," Edward said as a man looked up from his desk.

"Grand," the man said as he waved Tommy and Jacob toward him. They slowly made their way over. Usually, this would be the time Edward left to recruit more people, but this time he stood perfectly still. They filled out the recruitment paper and were rushed over to one of the physicians.

"Anything else, soldier?" the man at the table asked looking at Edward.

He chewed the inside of his cheek silently debating with himself.

"Yes sir, one more thing. I want to go too."

"Very well," the man smiled holding a pen up. Tommy looked at Edward, who simply ignored the look. He quickly filled out the form before he could second-guess himself and went into his physical. He focused his attention on the physician, making sure to not give any hint of his deafness away. When the three were declared fit they were asked a series of questions referring to riding horses and being able to do so when needed. They all answered with a strong 'yes' and listened on what was now expected of them.

They learned that they would be leaving by Wednesday from Paddington station to the southern part of England. Edward knew what was expected of him and where they would be leaving from.

"You two," the man pointed to the twins. "Lance Corporal Poole will be in charge of you until you reach France. Any further questions?"

"No sir," the twins answered before they were dismissed. The man turned to Edward and saluted.

"Welcome back, Lance Corporal."

Edward returned the salute with a smile and soon left the recruitment office.

"Care to join us for a beer?" Jacob asked.

"Maybe tomorrow. There's someone I need to talk to tonight," Edward replied. "I'll buy ya each one. Meet me in Piccadilly tomorrow around half six."

They nodded, and everyone went their separate ways. Suddenly this feeling of guilt Edward felt was lifted from his shoulders as a cool late autumn wind blew.

When he reached his flat, he found Vera already there waiting for him outside the building.

"I didn't have to work today," she said, standing on the steps.

"So you were going to sit outside till I got off?" Edward laughed as she nodded innocently. "Let's go out tonight," he sighed. She looked at him, scrunched her brows and took his hand.

"Sure. Is everything all right?" She looked nervously at him.

"Yeah." He squeezed her hand as they walked down the street in silence. Edward led her. He wanted to break the news to her in an easy fashion, but knew no way to do it. He walked in silence not knowing exactly where his own feet were taking him until they came to the restaurant from their first date. "My treat," he insisted, as the two walked into the restaurant. Vera smiled. They were shown to the same seat they had occupied over a year ago. Edward looked out the window again at the people passing down below in the streets.

"Something is clearly on your mind."

"Indeed something is, but maybe we shouldn't talk about it this second."

Vera sighed and looked at him crossed.

"You signed up those lads didn't you?"

"They came and found me, Vera, I can't turn any man away who wishes to sign."

"You wrote their lives away."

"No, I did no such thing."

"Well you assisted by taking them to the recruiters."

"They're going to be fine."

"How do you know that? You can't predict the future. You know what they're going into and yet you say they'll be fine?" she argued at a soft whisper. The waiter hesitated, but when he finally arrived Edward ordered a bottle of champagne.

"I just know they'll be fine."

"Pray tell, how are you so bloody sure."

"Because I'm going with them," he snapped as she sat back looking blank. Her stare transformed into shock and then to anger. She started to laugh a little.

"You're funny."

"I'm serious, Vera. We leave Wednesday morning from Paddington."

"I don't believe you."

"Vera, I'm not a coward."

"Why would you think you are?"

He pulled the feather out from his jacket and placed it on the table. She looked at it and scoffed. "Seriously?"

"Vera, it felt like a weight. I can't stay here while my friends die. This war is ending."

"So let it end."

"I want to end it. Vera, don't you see I'm going to fight for you, for the country."

"And the baby," she huffed, sitting back in her seat.

"Baby?" He smiled. "Baby?" He repeated his question as Vera nodded angrily. "You're positive?"

"I'm three weeks late," she whispered. She had a look of embarrassment on her face.

"Why are you just telling me now?" he asked, reaching for her hand. She shook her head and shrugged her shoulders. He was surprised she wasn't showing the same happiness he felt. He reached across the table and took her hand looking her dead in the eyes. "Vera, you know my word is always true, and I swear to you I will take care of you and the baby."

"And how can you if your dead?" she started to cry.

He squeezed her hand.

"I assure you, I'll come home." He fell silent, leaning back in his seat. She was fragile and weak. He feared now for her and the baby. His child grew inside her and he felt the urge to fight now more than ever. "I want you to go to Bourne," he instructed sternly.

She never looked up from the empty plates on the table.

"I want you to go to my home and wait for me there. My mother will take care of you, and she'll be thankful someone will be there to help her take care of my little brother and sister. I'll write to her and let her know you're coming."

Vera looked up agitated.

"And what happens when you don't return?"

"Then you'll have others to look over you." He closed his eyes, knowing he didn't want to say that. She shoved the seat back and made her way to the exit just as the waiter arrived with the champagne. "I'm sorry," Edward sighed.

He placed twenty bob on the table before leaving after her. When he reached the street, she was gone. Angry, he made his way back to his flat silently mumbling and cursing to himself.

***

Edward stood on the station platform in uniform overlooking the train. He found himself looking toward the entrance from time to time, hoping to see Vera. "What are you waiting for an invitation?" Tommy yelled from a nearby window. Edward waved him off and continued looking around.

"Come on, Vera," he whispered.

The train whistled and Edward looked at his pocket watch. It would leave in less than twenty minutes. Men leaned out of the train windows saying goodbye to their loved ones. After the second whistle blew, Edward climbed on the train and threw his bag on the rack above.

"Took you a while."

"Bugger off," Edward said, shoving Jacob.

"Hey, Lance Corporal, someone's here for you," Tommy said leaning out the window. Edward stood and looked out the window as Vera ran down the platform. She reached up as he grabbed her hand, leaning halfway out the window to reach her.

"We'll be waiting," she said placing her free hand on her stomach. "You come back to us, understand?"

"By the end of the year," he said jokingly, although there was only two and a half months left of the year.

"We'll meet you in Bourne," she added.

A small smile appeared on his face. The final whistle blew as a guard yelled for final departure. Edward looked toward the front as he watched soldiers running from their girls onto the train.

"Grab my legs," he instructed Tommy and Jacob as he pulled himself further out the window.

"What are you doing?" Vera laughed. Edward leaned down toward her. She reached as far as she could, standing on her toes to reach him.

Edward leaned down, grabbing the back of her neck he kissed her. Soldiers watched and cheered from inside the train while others cheered from the platform. They separated when the train began to move and Jacob and Tommy pulled him in.

"I'll see you soon. I love you," he called, waving with a big smile on his face.

She laughed and waved back. She told him she loved him, but over the sound of the train and those calling from the platform he couldn't hear her.

When Edward got back on the train, the men gathered around applauding him. He laughed and waved them away. Tommy said something, but he couldn't hear him.

"Come again, private?"

"When do we arrive in France?" Tommy asked again.

"Late tonight," Edward sighed. He leaned back in his seat closing his eyes and thinking of what waited for them. He wondered who would be there to greet them.

Chapter 19

Edward sat comfortably and prideful on Blood Stream's back. He looked over his shoulder from time to time, carefully watching the twins. They rode with Charlie, who seemed to be in full conversation with them. "So, over a year later and you couldn't stay away?" Liam laughed riding up on Edward's left side.

"Come again?" Edward asked, only catching the end of Liam's question. Liam repeated what he had said which caused Edward to chuckle. "Well I could, but I couldn't at the same time. So where are we going? Back to Arras?"

"Further south, we'll be in Cambrai soon enough." They stopped their horses for the evening. Both those new to battle and the veterans were exhausted. Edward took a look around. Many of the men that had joined them were unfamiliar, only a handful he recognized on sight. Charlie jumped down from his horse and marched toward Edward, extending his hand in greeting. But Edward was so happy that he pulled him into a hug instead.

"It's good to see you, both of you." Liam smiled a little before looking grim. "I'm assuming William is…"

"William died," Charlie said grimly. "Four months ago."

"What? How?"

"Stood up to look over the top. Shot right between the eyes," Liam sighed. "James died too."

"He had a strong head on him."

"Not when he returned from hospital," Liam said. His face was long and tired. Wrinkles formed, making that young and vigorous man Edward knew a year ago look far older. "He couldn't stop going on about how he wanted to go home. When Jerry sent over there artillery, he lost it."

"He didn't desert?"

"No. Shot himself." Edward looked at Liam, completely surprised. "Took his rifle under the chin and used his foot, God... we lose them by the day now."

"This damn war is going nowhere and taking so many good lives," Charlie sighed. "You shouldn't have returned."

"I couldn't stay behind any longer." Edward looked around the camp. The twins stood grooming their new horses while others scattered around the make shift facilities. Edward retrieved his journal from his pack and began writing while Charlie and Liam made some dinner. He felt guilt inside him wondering how many of the men he sent still lived. When the camp became silent they listened to the battles on the front line.

"We'll be there tomorrow," Edward said, making his way to the twins. He sat next to Tommy. The twenty-three-year-old sat quietly staring blankly at the distance. "We'll make it through, the three of us."

"Why are you so sure?"

"Because I know. I can feel it deep in my gut that this war is on the turning point. We are going to win this."

"I wish I could share your optimism. But forgive me I cannot."

"Tommy. Look around, tell me what you see."

"I see hills with poppies. I see a small farm, over there," he said pointing to a little barn with the lights still on.

"I see a land filled with hope waiting for liberation from Germany, and we're the only ones who can do that. Come here, both of you," he said looking past Tommy at Jacob. Edward stood up and made his way toward Blood Stream. The horse snorted at his approach and he pet the soft velvet nose of the horse. "Go in with the mindset of a horse."

"Blind and dumb?" Jacob quizzed.

"No. These creatures are far from dumb. They know to run away when they know they can't win. They can sense danger coming from any direction. This horse was my best friend's horse. I promised to take care of him. The day I lost my friend, I lost my own horse. I was told in hospital that Blood Stream was still standing over me when my men found me. This horse was loyal to me."

"So what are you saying?"

"I'm saying fight, even when your friends are falling around you, fight. When we reach the front tomorrow, the world you know will end. Follow orders. And don't get yourself shot. I won't be able to hear much and if I am unable to give an order, you listen to the next higher officer. Do I make myself clear?"

Without saying a word, the brothers both nodded. "Good, get some rest, you'll need it." Tommy and Jacob left Edward alone with his horse. He looked in Blood Stream's eyes before pressing his forehead to the horse's nose. Blood Stream nudged him back causing him to laugh. "Yeah, you too," he whispered.

***

Edward and those that joined him arrived in Cambrai by midday. Listening to the gunfire that came from the front line put a surge of pride in him. He looked at Tommy and Jacob and glanced at Liam and Charlie. "Men, it's been an honor fighting by your sides, in the past and present."

They entered the reserve lines. No face looked familiar. The further they reached the front line the more his nerves shook.

"Hold your arses!" Lieutenant Gyles shouted. Edward turned and saluted the Lieutenant.

"Lance Corporal Edward Poole reporting in," he shouted as Lieutenant Gyles smirked and returned the salute.

"What the hell are you doing here?" the lieutenant shouted as Edward leaned forward with his left ear.

"I couldn't sit back any longer. My friends needed me," he shouted back.

A shell exploded above them and everyone lowered themselves closer to the ground. Lieutenant Gyles patted Edward's shoulder as he caught a glimpse of Liam, Charlie, Tommy, and Jacob waiting for him. He pointed to the men behind him.

"Already making your squad?"

"We're ready for your orders, Lieutenant," Edward said as he and the Lieutenant began walking down the trench with Edward's men following behind. Edward made sure to stand at Gyles' right so he could catch any conversation. Another shell went off above them, and again they took cover.

When they reached the end of the trench, Edward gave the order to hold the line. Lieutenant Gyles saluted his squad before leaving. The noise around was deafening so he closed his eyes and tried focusing, but there was too much to focus upon.

Suddenly, the ground shook and over the trench a Mark IV tank came into view. Edward stared at the beast of a machine as the entire trench shook beneath its weight. He stood as the mammoth of steel passed over, watching as it traveled straight on for the German side.

"We'll have this won within a fortnight," Edward laughed looking at Tommy who held his rifle close to his chest. "Stay focused." Tommy nodded nervously as another shell exploded behind and around them.

***

The first night was much quieter than the first day. The rumble of tanks continued, but the artillery had let up. Edward could finally concentrate. He looked at his men already dirty from being in the trench for a day or longer. "Charlie, Liam will take the first rest."

"Sir?" Liam asked.

"You've been fighting a good fight, rest now." Charlie looked at Edward and then Liam.

Without further questions Liam and Charlie entered the small dugout before them.

"Tommy, start fortifying the trench over there, where it looks to be caving." Edward pointed to a section the trench that had splintered. He grabbed the periscope that lay against the trench wall and handed it to Jacob. "Keep an eye for any movement out there. Call me if you spot anything."

Jacob nodded and pressed himself against the wall of the trench, scanning no man's land.

Edward made his way to where Tommy stood digging in the trench and, grabbing his own entrenching tool, began digging with him. "We fight and work as one."

"How long are we going to do this for?"

"Don't ask," Edward laughed. "Just think of home. Farming on the land. Wait, you know nothing of farming," Edward joked as Tommy shoved him. Tommy looked past Edward at his brother, who was studying the landscape beyond their trench.

"I ought to be thanking you in a way."

"What for?" Edward grumbled as he shoveled mud from the land.

"Finding a way to get him in this war. He wouldn't shut the bloody hell up about it." Edward looked over his shoulder at Jacob. He looked like a child who had been given the world, young, strong, and full of will.

"There is always a loop hole in the systems. You just need to know where to look. Why do you think I took you to the recruitment office halfway across London?"

"Because there they didn't know us."

"Exactly, nor me." Tommy gave Edward a sideways glance. "I knew that recruitment office was linked to my old regiment, which is what we currently are in. I knew the recruitment office I usually brought people to would never allow me to resign up considering I was on honorary discharge. They knew I was deaf in one ear." Tommy looked at him in disbelief.

"I admit it is more dangerous for me to be here, but the less people who know the better. The only ones who do know are my old friends and you now."

"And the Lieutenant?"

"He knows, too. Now back to work, soldier." Edward dug with Tommy for the next several hours, ignoring any question his private had about his deafness or the past battles. He only responded with short grunted responses unless it was a question about their current situation.

They spent hours on the trench till they could no longer dig. At half past three, Charlie and Liam came out to relieve them. Jacob and Tommy entered the dugout to rest while Edward sat next to a small kettle.

"Why did you return?"

"I couldn't stay behind while the rest of you died."

"So you took the blessing of escape and threw it away," Liam said as Edward poured three cups of tea, handing one to each man.

"Some woman with a white feather..."

"The Order of the White Feather," Charlie and Liam said in unison. Edward looked up at them, sipping from his metal tin.

"Many men who have been coming have been given a white feather. Branded as cowards by the women back home," Liam said with a snarky tone.

"The feminists have good cause at times, but that's one of their worst ideas," Charlie sighed.

"Forcing men into feeling guilty for not signing up, only to send em to their deaths." Edward listened to the two go on about the Order of the White Feather. He wanted to learn more of how it started, but digging all night left him weak and exhausted. He finished his tea and went to the dugout to get some rest.

He only rested a little when a bombardment of shellfire jolted him awake. The dugout they lay in rumbled and shook, the dirt and dust falling from the ceiling.

"Get out!" he ordered Tommy and Jacob. The three quickly climbed out seeing shells exploding further down the line. The five men stood close to the trench wall as the shellfire continued, getting steadily closer.

Further down, the trench splintered and shattered as men died from debris or shrapnel. Edward looked over the top rifle ready as a line of German's started over the top. "Men to the ready!" he shouted, propping his rifle on the trench wall. "Take aim!" The machine guns of the allied sides fired first. "Hold, do not fire yet."

Liam, Charlie, and Tommy propped their weapons taking aim. "Jacob, take aim!" Edward demanded as the frightened man stood, fumbling with his rifle. "Damn it, private!" Edward jumped down from the trench ledge, grabbed Jacob and shoved him against the trench wall. "Take aim!" Jacob propped his rifle next to his brother's. Edward took his position again, the Germans only fifty yards from their line. "On my word!" he shouted over the sound of machine guns, artillery, and shouts of other men. He ignored the sounds and focused on the line that moved forward. Germans were already falling to the machine guns. "Fire!" The rifles fired, deafening Edward completely. "Reload and fire again!" He cocked the bolt and fired again as his men did the same. A few more Germans fell.

They continued to release round after round, but the Germans continued with their attack. "Liam prepare for breach." Edward looked over his shoulder as he watched Liam jump down to a smaller machine gun. He prepped the weapon, loaded and readied it down one of the empty passageways of the trench. "Keep firing, only fall back behind Liam when they're ten yards away!" Edward instructed the three on the wall. He jumped down and grabbed his canteen, making sure it was filled he handed it to Liam. "To cool it down," he said.

"They're coming!" Tommy shouted as the three men jumped from the wall preparing themselves behind Edward and Liam who had the machine gun ready.

Chapter 20

9 November, 1918

The news is impossible to comprehend. As I sit here writing, I cannot believe what Lieutenant Gyles has just told me. I should inform the lads soon that in two days time this war will end?

No. At this time this is a rumor.

We've heard news of a peace negotiation but I won't believe it until it happens. War will come to an end, eventually. We've been fighting for so long that I will only believe it when it happens. If I received this information before that attack last month I would refuse to believe it. But now it seems like it could happen.

I'm putting too much faith into a rumor. The Jerry we eliminated from this earth with our rifles and machine guns. God, it's almost over. I almost regret my orders of using the machine gun, but it was our lives or theirs and I was not going to lose any more of my men.

Liam took them all out. Those that survived retreated shortly after entering the trench. Those who could escape it. I believe the German side was even taken a few days back by some of the

Canadian forces. All this will end as I promised
Vera. I would be home by the end of the year. I only
said it to keep her spirits high. I wonder if Andrew
or Gavin have heard word of this end to the war
yet? Or is it simply myself that knows? I heard a
rumor from Charlie yesterday that we would be
making advancements on their lines in the next day
or two. If this truce is to happen, I doubt Charlie's
words to be true.

Now we must sit and wait. Hold our trench until the
eleventh and see. No matter how many times I write
this, I cannot believe it. I need a good cup of char
and a cushy spot for the next two days. Keep one
eye on the wall and another on sights of home. I've
been away from Vera for only a month but it feels
like a year. I regret none of it. I am ready to make
sure that each of my men return home. My heart
pounds at the excitement as strong as it pounded the
very first day I enlisted a year and a half ago.

After seeing this place, no man should ever
have to live through this again, I do pray for it to be
the War to End All Wars. I guess it's time for my
daily checks and marks and to inform then men of
what will happen in two days time, if it will happen.

11 November, 1918 9:30 AM

I've given the order to my men that there will be no
firing of any weapon after 11 AM today. This war is
ending. Finally! They don't seem too happy with
my order and I can see that they still do not believe
it. I'll need Lieutenant Gyles to explain it to them.
Yesterday was an easier day of artillery firing back
and forth. No side made an advance on the other.
We are so close to the end casualties are not worth
it. The tanks are probably the loudest thing on the

battlefield. They are a sight to see. I find them just as fascinating, if not more so, than the aeroplanes. These machines are simply our artillery on wheels, except they can travel on nearly every terrain and obstacle. No wonder Gavin worked on them for so long, he learned every part by building these things, knowing how they work well before they could.

I still remember what he said before we signed up to enlist. "Cowards die many times before their deaths, the valiant never taste of death but once." I believe I was true to this. Never once did I encounter my own death to being a coward. Never did I lead myself down the path of the coward. I stood strong. I stood for the name and sake of my King and Country. I was made a Lance Corporal at the age of 18 simply because most men listened to me. If this war has taught me anything, it was that I succumbed to nothing. I stood my ground when needed and I took complete control.

Like that boy we found hiding in the house outside of Arras. Why didn't I simply kill the German? Why did I let him live? I let him live because he was young. Shooting him there while he cowered in the corner of the room like a dog would have been murder. I may have blood on my hands, but not that of the innocent. The blood that stains my hands now is that of my enemy, another man trying to take my life for the same beliefs as mine, a pride of country and honor.

We are so driven by pride. Some let it go to their heads. Those are the ones who die first and are remembered last. Those who fought with valour are the ones who will be remembered when this is passed. This war will never be forgotten. Our names will never be forgotten. Until tomorrow we must still fight our enemy. Then the real victors will rise.

11 November, 1918 11:30 AM

It happened half an hour ago. I may return to no man's land shortly. Some of the Germans have also stepped outside of their trenches. We have nothing to celebrate the end of the war with except for some biscuits. Charlie cried with excitement as Liam hugged him. It was a sight to see.

The fear of death is nowhere. I was watching my pocket watch for the last ten minutes of the war counting down to the last second. At the strike of eleven I ordered Tommy, Jacob, Charlie, Liam, and anyone in ear shot to ceasefire. The sound of silence fell upon us and I could have sworn I smiled. "That's it lads, the war is over," I said loud enough for everyone to hear.

I didn't believe the words coming out of my own mouth. The war had ended, four years and the fighting just stopped like that. I wonder how they're celebrating back home?

I was one of the first to climb out of the trench. Some of the lads were yelling at me, but the war was over according to a treaty signed two hours before 11 AM. The eleventh hour of the eleventh day of the eleventh month has a ring to it. This day is going to go down in history. Then, as I stood in no man's land, I spotted a German who climbed from his trench. I couldn't believe I was walking toward a man who was once my enemy.

"Do you speak English, sir?" I asked as he cleared his throat.

"Only a little," he replied. I was surprised how well it sounded. "Cigarette?" I nodded and took the fag he offered me. I pulled my matches out and lit his then mine before taking a long, deep inhale of smoke. Soon, a handful of men from both sides joined us. I guess many were afraid of getting in trouble for fraternizing with the enemy, but were we still enemies now the war was over? This German proved to me he was not.

I can't believe the war has ended.

13 November, 1918

It's been two days since the end of the war, and the first full day my men and I haven't been sitting in a trench. I have received news from Lieutenant Gyles that we will remain in France a little longer to ensure the country's safety. The German lines have started retreating back to their boarders as order of the treaty. This is so exciting, my heart is pounding with joy. I long to see the day of spending it with Vera and only having to worry about the farm.

I took Blood Stream out for a ride today. And according to my commanding officer, I am allowed to return home with him. Considering my position, I'll be able to keep Alf's promise after all. I spent a good hour and a half riding along a river visiting small towns, some of which had been abandoned due to bombings. It was really a sight to see. I'm simply chuffed to bits right now. I'll be a father soon, I'll keep a promise I made a long time ago, and I finally get to return home. Home is in my grasp. Soon enough, when things are secured and France is completely safe, we'll be leaving.

-Lance Corporal Edward Jacob Poole

Chapter 21

Edward slept, the soothing sound of the train
rocking him gently. He served his time at war and
his time on clean up. Four months after the signing
of the armistice he was finally being sent home. His
mind was still and peace was deep within him. He
thought of nothing and dreamed of nothing. He was
secure in his seat and all was coming to an end.
Tommy and Jacob Atkins remained in France,
Charlie got off in London, and so did Liam, to catch
another train. Their time in France had finally come
to an end.

Edward looked forward to nothing except
his family and the farm. After another stop at a
station, he finally woke up. The train was somewhat
full, mostly with soldiers like him returning home.
An American sat across from him reading the paper.
"Did I wake you?" he asked as Edward yawned.

"No, I just wake every time the train stops,"
Edward laughed. The American nodded. "You're a
long way from home," he added, as the American
folded his paper.

"Sort of. I got some relatives up north I
thought I'd visit before going back to America.
Where are you off to?"

"Home, finally. Bourne." The American nodded. "Got my girl waiting with my family."

"Yeah? So do I," the American said, pulling a picture from his chest pocket. "That's her." Edward took the photo and looked at a model-like woman posing in the picture.

"She's pretty," he said politely, handing the picture back before taking a photo of Vera out. "Photos don't do her justice," he said handing the picture to the man who sat across from him.

"Are you kidding? She's gorgeous."

"Cheers," Edward smiled, taking the photo back, "that was taken a few weeks before I left the second time. She's probably grown in belly since I've been gone."

"You left her with child?" The American slapped Edward's knee jokingly as both men chuckled. "That's one way to get a lady to stay with you."

"That's for sure." The two men talked about their homes Edward learned a little more of a country he knew little of and swore to visit if he ever decided to cross the Atlantic. In his mind he knew the possibilities of that ever happening were slim, focusing all his time on the farm would hardly produce enough money to get a ticket to travel across the Atlantic by sea.

Edward said his goodbye as the train pulled into the Bourne station and looked out the window of the rather empty platform. He and a few others stepped off the train, no one he recognized. Walking further down the platform, he watched as one of the guards carefully pulled Blood Stream from a transportation car. The man handed Edward the reins.

"Come on, let's go see where everyone is,"
he whispered, pulling the horse down the platform.
He was surprised no one was there to greet him.
He'd sent the letter home a week before he left. He
started to wonder if it was even delivered.

Climbing atop Blood Stream, his pack on his
back, Edward gave the great horse a little kick to
get it moving. Trotting through the town he found
people cheering and hugging their loved ones. The
town was coming to life finally. He supposed word
had not reached them that they would be arriving
today, judging from the looks of surprise on those
that greeted the soldiers.

"Eddie!"

Edward pulled hard on Blood Stream's reins
as the horse struggled to a stop. He looked over his
shoulder as a clean-cut blonde man ran toward him.
Edward jumped down from Blood Stream's back.
"Look at you, mate!"

"And yourself, Gav. I hardly recognized
you," Edward said patting his friend's shoulder.
"Can ya believe it? Look how far we've come."

"Let me buy ya a beer."

"Not now Gav."

"Come on, your twentieth only happens
once."

"I need to get home first. I'll be back
tonight."

"You can go home later, one pint, to
celebrate the end of the war."

"Later, all right."

Gavin looked annoyed.

"Fine, we'll go to your house then get a
pint." Edward could tell his friend hadn't changed
at all from the war. He was still upbeat and jolly and
desperate for a drink. The two walked shoulder-to-

shoulder Gavin on the left, Edward on the right. They discussed their version of the war, sparing each other the hardest parts.

Edward shared how he became deaf in the right side, and Gavin showed Edward were a piece of jagged metal from a bomb sliced open his shoulder. Edward smoked nearly the entire walk, only to throw the fag away before reaching his house.

When they arrived, Edward tied Blood Stream to a post before walking to the front door. There, the two men stood for a little over a minute, Edward's fist a few inches from the door.

"Knock, already," Gavin laughed nudging his friend. Finally Edward pounded on the door, his heart echoing in his head.

Suddenly, Lily stood in the open doorway. She looked a little more mature to Edward. The nine-year-old instantly leapt toward her brother nearly tackling him in the process. After putting her down, she disappeared into the house.

"Mama, Mama, Vera!" her voice echoed through the farmhouse. Edward and Gavin stepped in, closing the door behind them. The smell of fresh made biscuits filled their nostrils.

Vera stood at the top of the steps panting holding her big belly and smiling widely as Edward dashed up the stairs.

"You're home?" she asked between kisses.

"Mama, Vera!" Lily continued to scream.

"How's the baby?" he whispered, placing his hand on her large stomach.

"Healthy, very healthy." They couldn't stop smiling at each other.

"Gavin," Edward's mother said in surprise. "Well don't you look dashing?" Edward looked over his shoulder, rolling his eyes as Gavin adjusted his military jacket pridefully. His mother looked up the steps nearly in awe. Slowly he walked down with Vera right behind him. "Let me look at you," she said adoringly. "I wish I knew you were coming home today," she gasped covering her mouth, "we would have had a little birthday…"

"Mother, no," he laughed kissing her forehead. "I don't need a party. Let's just have a quiet evening."

"Okay."

He kissed her forehead again before wrapping his arm around Vera. "Where's Will?" Edward looked around.

"In the garden," his mother answered with a bigger smile. "Why not go and see him?"

Nodding, he let go of Vera and walked through the house to the back door. He found Will right where his mother said.

"Edward!" Will shouted. Edward stood in surprise as Andrew turned around with Will on his shoulders. Andrew put Will down and the little boy ran across the garden to hug his older brother.

"Welcome home," Andrew said calmly. The two men stood silently before embracing.

"I thought you died."

"I'm pretty hard to kill," Andrew laughed.

"Well, write once in a while dammit." They laughed and soon walked back into the house.

"God has blessed me, I can die in peace," his mother said joyfully as the girls laughed.

"We can all die in peace," Vera said, soothingly grabbing Edward's hand.

"All right, can we get a drink now?" Gavin called from the doorway as Edward rolled his eyes.

"Yes, fine, yes we can get a drink now," he yelped as Gavin and Andrew walked for the door.

"Be home for dinner?"

"Of course, mother," he answered kissing her forehead once more. He grabbed Vera by the hand and dragged her to the door. "Oh did I mention you were coming?" She laughed as the four of them left the house. Placing his arm on Vera's shoulder she took his hand, listening to the men share their stories.

Outside the pub was a lot quieter, and so that Edward didn't have to strain to hear the conversation they waited there. Gavin and Andrew brought them a beer and they continued with their stories, holding nothing back. They shared the fearful parts and the glorious parts of war. Edward learned that Gavin was also at Cambrai the day of the war ended. He wondered how far were they from actually meeting. Andrew told them how he took his plane out for a relaxing flight not having to worry about shooting or being shot at. Vera was visiting her parents the day the war ended. She shared how it was a chilling surprise to hear the bells in the church steeple finally ringing.

"Oh, the city was almost like one big party," she said with a great big smile. "Almost like the biggest party the world has seen. My God you could hardly move. That's how crowded the streets were."

"Did you go out?"

"No, but my sister did. She had loads of fun. I was more concerned with the baby," Vera answered honestly, holding her stomach with one hand and the beer with the other. "What were you lads doing?"

"I told ya, went on up in my airplane," Andrew laughed.

"I shared a fag with a German," Edward spoke up as everyone looked at him.

"Wait, you're serious?" Andrew asked as Edward nodded.

He then went on to share what happened when he received rumors of the armistice papers being signed and the ceasefire the day it happened. He told them of how he was one of the first to climb out of the trench and walk no man's land without the worry of being shot.

The conversation continued with them talking of the days that followed the end. "All right, all right," Edward finally said. "In all honesty, we made it, some in better condition than others. But there were a great many of our friends who didn't. And so let's just take a moment to remember them." The group became silent.

"For those that died and gave their lives fighting strong," Gavin spoke up.

Andrew raised his glass, "For the memories we still hold of them."

"May they continue to live on as long as we stand," Edward added.

"And may the children of our children's children remember what happened these past four years," Vera said with her hand on her belly.

About the Author:
Dan Heiser is a born raised Floridian. He has been into studying history for as long as he could remember. He spends most of his time researching European history. If he isn't researching, he is spending time with his family, playing video games, or working on homework. He will graduate at the end of the year from Full Sail University with a Bachelor's in Game Design.

www.ingramcontent.com/pod-product-compliance
Lightning Source LLC
Chambersburg PA
CBHW071909220626
47052CB00002B/279